The Neighbor, The O'Connells
Paperback Copyright © 2020 Lorhainne Ekelund
Editor: Talia Leduc

All rights reserved.
ISBN-13: 9798515301613

Give feedback on the book at:
lorhainneeckhart@hotmail.com

Twitter: @LEckhart
Facebook: AuthorLorhainneEckhart

Printed in the U.S.A

Secrets and Lies in a Small Town

From a *NY Times & USA Today* bestselling author: Park ranger Ryan is shocked when Jenny, a one-night stand from years ago, moves to his Montana town with her troublesome daughter, Alison. But he can't resist the pull he feels toward her — especially once Alison goes missing and the truth about her daughter's real identity comes out…

Park ranger Ryan is one of the six O'Connell siblings in Livingston, raised by an independent mom who has been a rock to him. He has a career he loves, and up until six weeks ago, he lived a comfortable life. When a new neighbor moves in and disturbs the quiet peace of the area, bringing with her a daughter who's walking trouble.

Right now, the gorgeous Jenny isn't too interested in making friends, but despite her cool façade, as Ryan gets to know her, he can't fight an idiotic need to try to ease the pain he sees her trying to hide. At the same time, he knows deep down that both mother and daughter have a secret, and if he were smart, he would listen to his brother's warning and walk away.

But Ryan can't resist the pull he feels toward Jenny— especially once Alison goes missing and the truth about her daughter's real identity comes out.

Chapter 1

More or less, Livingston was a quiet town—except for the person next door, the supreme a-hole he had yet to meet.

Ryan O'Connell's scale of assholes went from your average pain in the ass, to the lying, cheating dirty dog, to the class A supreme asshole who didn't give a fuck about anyone and conceivably embraced being said asshole, considering the intolerable noise from next door.

Ryan wasn't in the mood to deal with yet another asshole today as he dragged on a pair of gray sweats after toweling off from a cool shower in the August Montana heat.

The stereo thumped from the Kunkels' house next door. Actually, scratch that. Althea Kunkel had been a sweet old busybody, always trying to fix Ryan up. She had been the ideal neighbor, though she had always invaded his privacy and his peace of mind, waking him at seven a.m. on Sundays with freshly baked cinnamon rolls. At times, he'd been forced to sneak into his own house after parking up the street so she wouldn't know he was home.

She was now six feet under, and Ryan missed her.

Good neighbors were hard to find.

He would've given anything to have that meddling busybody back instead of the unnamed scumbag who'd recently moved in. Every night for the past three weeks, his new neighbor had incessantly cranked the music so loud that the thump of the bass bounced the only piece of artwork, a painting of dogs smoking and playing poker, that he had on his vibrant white walls. It had been a joke from his sister Suzanne, one of Livingston's three fulltime firefighters, and he swore she hadn't expected him to hang it in such a prominent spot in the house.

That was just one of those things they did on their birthdays, really digging in and competing to find the perfect gift the other would hate. But Ryan was determined always to have the last laugh, and he'd hung the painting in the living room for everyone to see. He liked dogs and found humor in it, and he could see how much it annoyed his sister every time she stopped by.

"Goddamn asshole," he said under his breath as he jogged down his stairs, barefoot and pissed, ready to lay out the dos and don'ts of being a good neighbor as the annoying thump continued.

He pulled open his front door, wanting only peace and quiet, a beer, and an hour or two in front of his idiot box to watch the episode of *Survivor* saved on his PVR. He stepped out onto the covered porch, the sky dark except for the streetlights, and strode across his overgrown grass, taking in the rusty Hyundai parked in his neighbor's driveway.

Across the street, Ham Johnson, bald and fortyish, with three kids and a wife who visited her sister in Idaho every other week, which was when his girlfriend would stay over, was standing on his front porch and watching. Yeah, Ham was just another asshole, but he lifted his hand in a wave and walked back into his house.

Ryan's neighbor's two-story craftsman was identical to his, with now wilting daisies in the flower boxes. He took in the lit house, the closed door, and the noise, which was nearly deafening as he stepped onto the front porch and fisted his hand. He lifted it to the screen and yanked it open with a barely audible squeak, then pounded on the door. "Hey, shut it down!" he yelled. He could be loud when he wanted to, but he was having trouble hearing himself, considering the music was still thumping.

It was a tune he knew well, "Bad to the Bone."

"Fucking asshole," he said under his breath, then pounded the door again with his fist, louder. He kept pounding until the music suddenly stopped, and he could finally hear his heart thumping, the pull of his breath, and a noticeable ring in the air as the quiet of night was no longer disrupted.

One, two, three… He heard the footsteps and then nothing, forcing himself to listen, as he thought for sure the asshole had stopped on the other side of the door. He waited for it to open when the light suddenly flicked off, not just the inside light but the porch light too, leaving him standing in the dark. Like, what the fuck?

"Hey, open the damn door!" he said and pounded on the door again. The neighbors' dogs were now barking and doors were opening, as if he was now the problem. "You think I don't know you're in there? Like, what are you, two years old? Open the damn door."

He was positive his neighbor was standing just on the other side, the fucking little coward. Now he had no intention of walking away. "Look, I'm not leaving until we talk and set some ground rules…"

The light flicked on, and he heard the deadbolt click

and watched as the doorknob turned and the door opened. He was staring into the deep brown eyes of a girl who was maybe sixteen, seventeen. She had shoulder-length black hair and wore black eye shadow, a low-cut green army tank, and cut-off shorts that left nothing to the imagination. She also had a nose ring.

For a second, he was speechless. She said nothing.

"I live next door," he finally said. "I'm your neighbor. Do you have any idea how loud your music was? It was so loud I couldn't hear myself think." He gestured next door with his thumb and took in the way she stared at him, her eyes lingering on his naked chest. Shit, he'd just stepped out of the shower and pulled on a pair of sweats. He hadn't bothered with anything else.

"Sorry," was all she said as she moved to close the door.

He slapped his hand on it. "Whoa, hang on a second. You know, it's not as if this is a first offence. This had been going on every night. Who all lives here? Is this, like, some frat house or something?" He took her in and could see the teenage attitude emerging. She was likely going to tell him to go fuck himself.

"What's it to you?" she said. Her eyes went right to his hand pressed to the door, holding it so she couldn't slam it in his face. In that moment, he realized how she could've taken it.

"Look, is your mom or dad here?" he said. She hadn't told him anything about who lived there, not that he could remember seeing anyone.

"Nope, just me," she said and didn't pull her gaze from him.

He had to fight the urge to laugh. "So you live here by yourself? A little young, aren't you?"

She slid her hand up the door frame and cocked her

hip in a teasing motion that had him pulling his hand away and stepping back. "Depends on what you like," she said.

He wondered if his eyes bugged out, and he glanced over his shoulder. "Cut the crap, kid. Don't…" he started, but just as he did so, he heard a car and saw the flashing lights of a cruiser as it parked out front. "You called the cops?"

She just shrugged, and he thought he saw the hint of a smile. In that second, he knew what the teen, whose name he still didn't know, had done. This was a girl who could cause him some serious trouble. He should've called the cops first!

"Oh, I'm so glad you got here when you did, officer," she said. "I didn't know what to do. My mom's not here, and this man won't leave. He threatened me and scared me, pounding on the door…"

Ryan couldn't pull his eyes from what seemed like an actress pulling off the perfect scene, and even her expression seemed to be that of a truly scared girl. He heard the creak of the step and took only a second to glance to the deputy now standing beside him, his hands on his belt. The man had the same O'Connell blue eyes he did, his dark wavy hair in the same cop cut he always wore. It was none other than his younger brother, who placed a hand on his shoulder.

"Are you for real, kid?" Ryan snapped.

"Well, aren't you going to arrest him?" the kid said accusingly, and he wondered for a second if this was a joke. The look on her face was all the reality check he needed.

"Care to explain, Ryan?" said Marcus O'Connell.

Just then, Ryan spotted the headlights of a small Jeep Patriot that was pulling in behind the rusty Hyundai.

"Wish I could," he said. "Came over because of the damn noise, a stereo, and now you're here. She called the cops?" He couldn't figure out when, maybe while she was avoiding answering the door.

"What's going on here?" said a woman emerging from the Jeep. She had dark hair and wore a baggy sweatshirt and a jean skirt that stopped at her knees, and she was carrying what looked like a grocery bag. Damn, she looked familiar. "Alison, what's going on? What did you do now?"

She was pretty—no, cute, slender. She had one of those faces that wouldn't get lost in a crowd, and he saw the spark of recognition when she saw him. Nothing friendly. He had to rack his brain to figure out where he knew her from.

"I'm Ryan O'Connell. I live next door," he said, and he actually held out his hand to the woman, who was now on the first step. For a second, he didn't think she'd shake it, but she did. Small hand, firm grip—and untrusting eyes. She said nothing, and he didn't miss the glance to his brother.

"Your music was so loud I couldn't hear myself think," he explained. "I came over here because it's been a nightly thing. I take it you're one of her parents?"

The woman pulled her hand from his and flicked her gaze to the teen in the doorway. Yup, definitely the angry mom look. "I'm so sorry," she said, then looked to the teen. "I told you no loud music! I apologize and can assure you it won't happen again."

"Well, I'm not here about the noise," Marcus said. "This young lady called 911 and said there was an intruder trying to break in, that she was home alone… We were just trying to get to the bottom of it when you showed up. I take it you live here?"

Ryan moved back and leaned against the post to watch.

"Yes, sorry. I'm Jennifer—Jenny, and this is my daughter, Alison." She handed off the paper bag to her daughter.

"You called the cops? What were you thinking?" Her voice squeaked, and he wondered whether this was something her daughter did often.

He glanced to his brother, who only shook his head. He wondered how many times Marcus had to deal with this kind of thing.

"He was being a dick, pounding on the door," Alison said. She didn't even try to pretend that she hadn't just made up a big lie. Ryan had heard of neighbors from hell, but he'd never expected to have one. He stood with his arms crossed over his naked chest, still trying to think of how he knew Jenny.

"You don't call the cops!" she said. "Seriously, Alison… Go unpack the groceries."

"Just hang on a second, here," Marcus said. "Calling 911 for kicks is a serious offense. At the same time, if I'm called out here because of noise, for example, your music cranked too loud, I'm going to fine you, because that's a problem."

Alison was holding the grocery bag and dragged her gaze to her mom, who appeared barely old enough to have a teenage daughter.

"I can assure you it won't happen again," Jenny said. "I will have a talk with my daughter and see to it that she behaves herself."

He noted the edge in her voice. That was the same tone his own mom had used on each of them when they misbehaved, pulling them aside alone at home for a talk they didn't want to have. There was fun mom, and then there was angry grounded-for-life mom. He could see this teen was getting the latter.

"So, then, the music…" he started.

Jenny lifted her hands, shaking her head. "It will stop,

like right now, and I'm sorry for the trouble my daughter caused."

Alison had already walked away, seeming completely unaffected at having a cop call her out. She was trouble with a capital T. He wondered if he should also give Jenny a heads-up on how her daughter had been toying with him and offering herself up to him.

"Is that all?" she asked. So much for any friendly neighborly talk. He was still trying to figure out how they knew each other and when they'd met.

"Guess so," he said. "Music's off, so the neighborhood should be happy. Oh, and you may want to keep your daughter on a short leash," he added as he stepped away from the post and down the steps. He stopped at the bottom, taking in the withering look his brother dragged over to him. Finally, Ryan said, "I'm trying to place it. Seems we've met. You look familiar."

She actually made a rude noise and crossed her arms. "So you don't remember?" she said.

He could feel his brother taking him in. "I'm great with faces, but I meet a lot of people in my line of work as a ranger. We meet on the trail or someplace in town or something?"

She seemed unimpressed. "Or something," she replied, and the way she said it oozed with sarcasm. She gestured to him. "Is this how you always dress, half naked, flaunting that perfect chest?"

Damn, her eyes were the same dark brown as the girl's, and he didn't miss the anger simmering below the surface.

"Just got out of the shower, and this is all I managed to pull on," he said. "Word of advice, Jenny: We're neighbors. It would be better to get along, and so far, you're not off to a great start."

He just couldn't help himself, and he wasn't sure what

the amused grin on his brother's face was about as Jenny narrowed her eyes, lifted her middle finger to him, and then stepped into the house and shut the door.

"Wow, you really have a way with women," Marcus said with a laugh.

Ryan just stepped down and took in the house a nice old woman had once lived in. God damn it, did he miss her. "It's a gift," he said, then lifted his hand to his brother as he cut across the grass, still barefoot. "See you at Mom's tomorrow."

"Hey, Ryan, word of advice?" Marcus called out.

He turned, resting his hands on his hips, not saying anything, knowing his brother had something on his mind.

"Next time, call me first," Marcus said. "Seen this before, and it ain't pretty. Remember, your territory's the woods, the park. Mine is this town. If a young girl calls the cops and makes up a story, a stupid schmuck could walk right into it and land in jail. It never ends well for the stupid schmuck, so don't let that be you." Marcus let out a sigh and shook his head. "She's trouble," he added. "Steer clear—and it's your turn to bring the beer tomorrow."

Ryan watched as his brother climbed into his cruiser, flicked off the still flashing lights, and drove away. He wasn't sure what made him look back to the house next door, but when he did, he was positive the girl was watching him from the upstairs window.

Chapter 2

"So what you're saying is this isn't your vehicle, and you didn't know you had to have a license to operate it in the park, and insurance, and actual tires?" Ryan said as he took in the two good ol' boys who had been ripping around the park in a souped-up pickup.

They had said their names were Bob and Darren. Bob shrugged, while Darren just stared at him with dark eyes as if still trying to figure out what his story was.

"Words, please, or do you not speak English?" Ryan said. "Again, I'm going to ask you one more time, any weapons on you or in the truck?"

"It's not as if it's a real road or anything," Darren said. He had to be at least five inches shorter than Bob. "Got a pistol, is all, for protection. I'm entitled to have a gun."

"And where is this pistol? You have it on you, or is it in the truck?" Ryan rested his hand on his heavy belt, feeling his holstered revolver. He'd lost count of the times he'd felt the need to reach for it. He was starting to get that feeling again.

"Glovebox, right? That's where you said you shoved it?" said Bob, who seemed unusually nervous.

Darren just stared at him and nodded. "Yeah, that's right, just a harmless little pistol."

"You two weren't also shooting out the window, were you? Or do you need a minute to change your story? Some hikers called in about a tireless truck screeching through the park, firing off a gun. I want both of you to lift your shirts and turn around right now," he snapped and waited, not expecting an answer.

Darren lifted his grimy white T-shirt, and Bob followed. Ryan scanned their white bellies and gestured for them to turn around, his other hand resting on the butt of his gun. He took in the pistol shoved in the back of Darren's baggy jeans and reached for it, pulling it out.

"Okay, link your fingers together, hands on your heads. Lie to me again and I'll cuff both of you. You forget that you were carrying a gun, or were you planning on pulling it on me? If I search your truck, what am I going to find?"

"No, sir," said Darren, shaking his head. His thick arms were sunburned, with a scratch on one forearm. "Listen, I just forgot it was there, is all. Thought I'd stuck it in the glovebox. Simple mistake. And it's just junk in the truck, not mine. Borrowed the truck from a friend, so don't know what all he's got in there."

Ryan checked the gun, seeing it was loaded with one in the chamber, and he didn't miss the scent of gunpowder, a sign it had recently been fired. He emptied the bullets and tucked the gun in his waistband at the small of his back, feeling the midday sun beating down on him. Beads of sweat dripped down his spine, and his damp short-sleeved dark shirt clung to his back. "Right now, I want you both to pull your wallets from your back pockets and show me your IDs." He didn't pull off his shades as both did so.

"Told ya, though, I forgot my license," Darren said. He was missing one of his lower front teeth. He appeared to be the older one, early thirties, whereas Bob was tall and lanky, mid-twenties, give or take. Ryan didn't buy anything they were saying. It was just that feeling he got when he knew someone was hiding something.

"Right, and you think I haven't heard that before? Open up your wallets. I want to see something with your names on it."

They both gave an awkward shuffle, and he took in the truck. Both doors were open, but he had blocked their exit by parking his four by four across the trail. When people saw him standing in front of his rig, cutting off their escape, it was always the same. These assholes figured they could do whatever they wanted in his park, believing it was their personal playland. Only once had he had to pull his gun on a driver to get him to stop.

Darren opened his wallet first, and Ryan could see the cards that filled the slots. He pulled out a Montana license, expired, with the name Dirk Hoskins. Sweat lined his brow. His dark greasy hair hung to his shoulders, and it was thin and balding in front.

"Look, we weren't causing no harm," Bob said. "It's not as if it's a real road, anyway. Just having some fun and blowing off steam, you know." He actually laughed as he said it, then pulled out an Idaho license with the name Ronald Steele.

Ryan glanced at the photos. Just the bugged-out expression in both showed the resemblance. "Hate to tell both of you this, but driving an unregistered vehicle in the park isn't allowed. And your way of blowing off steam could have killed someone. Let me guess: You forgot your license was in your wallet? One valid, one expired. You're both in deep shit."

Darren, or rather Dirk, shrugged.

"So explain this to me, Bob and Darren. Why are your names listed on these licenses as Dirk and Ronald?"

Ronald swallowed.

"So which is it, is the license fake, or did you just lie to a federal officer and give me a false name?" Ryan said. The expressions on their faces said everything. "Okay, let me help you out here before you dig yourselves in any deeper. I'm going to run your licenses, and the best option is to be straight with me, because if you lie to me one more time, you'll find yourselves cuffed and tossed in the back, then behind bars. I can come up with a dozen charges just off the top of my head."

"Okay, okay, didn't mean to lie, sir," Dirk said. "We weren't hurting nobody, just having some fun. It's just the park, the trails, not a real road…"

"Hate to tell you this, but you can get in a shitload of trouble for driving in a park, and you do need to have a properly registered vehicle, with papers and insurance and a valid driver's license. Then there's shooting off a gun in a national park…" He took in both the men, wondering if they'd keep arguing.

"Well, sir, I'm sorry," Dirk said. "We didn't realize. Can you let us off with a warning?"

He just took in the men, seeing another two who fit on his asshole scale, then shook his head, opened up the back of his four by four, and gestured inside. "Nope. Climb in. I'll give you a ride back to the station, where I'll write up your fines. The truck will be towed in, and you can tell your story again before a judge."

It was after five when he pulled up in front of the one-story bungalow where he'd grown up. Looked like some of his siblings were already there. He parked behind Owen's white cargo van, emblazoned with the logo of his plumbing company. Suzanne's work-in-progress red 1970 MGB was in the driveway behind Karen's practical four-door Honda. He stepped out of his rig just as Marcus pulled up in his cruiser, and he reached for two cases of beer in his back seat, one the stout his sister preferred and the other the light ale he and Marcus always went for.

"Heard you nailed those assholes ripping up the park," Marcus said. "Aren't they the same ones who've been causing all that ruckus out there over the last few weeks?"

Ryan handed off one of the cases and shoved the back door closed. "Not sure, maybe. Should've seen their faces when they saw me standing there. Damn near crapped their pants. It was fantastic." He laughed. "But at least now they'll think twice about heading into the park."

Especially considering the fines he'd slapped on them. Ryan and Marcus strode across the lawn, which had been littered with bikes more than a decade ago. His mom had just painted the front door a vibrant red.

"Just another asshole, right?" Marcus added.

Ryan wanted to roll his eyes, but he grunted instead as his brother headed first through the door. He could smell garlic from the roast beef he knew their mom was cooking. The game was on TV, and voices came from the kitchen as he took in his image in the mirrored coat closet that greeted everyone the minute they walked through the door. Yeah, his ranger's uniform was dusty, and his mom would tell him he needed a haircut.

He wiped his black boots and went down the two steps into the front room, seeing his brother Luke on the sofa, his long dark hair tied back in a ponytail. His blue O'Connell eyes were filled with an odd watchfulness that followed Ryan's every move.

"Toss me one of those beers," Luke said.

Ryan rested the case on the sofa table, ripped open the top, and lifted out two of the cold ales. He handed one to Luke, who always sat in the same spot when they visited his mom: the corner of the sofa in the corner of the room, with the wall behind him.

"You go out today?" Ryan asked. Luke was home for nine days on leave from the military—special forces, he knew, but where exactly he and his team had been, he didn't. That was what they didn't talk about.

"Yup. Montana State is behind." Luke gestured to the TV and downed half the beer. Okay, so they were still at that point. It would be another day or two before Luke would get off the sofa and have a real conversation.

"Hey, heard you had some trouble last night," his mom said as she strode out of the kitchen in light blue capris and a blue tank top. She was still slim and stylish, with short dark hair. She set a stack of plates on the dining room table.

"Oh, and who did you hear that from?" Ryan said. It was a ridiculous question, considering Marcus just couldn't help himself from sharing everything with their mom. He always had.

"Trouble? You, Ryan?" Suzanne added with a ton of sarcasm. She was in baggy shorts and an oversized T-shirt, carrying one of the stouts he'd brought.

"Just a problem with a neighbor that should now be rectified," he said—that was, if the mom actually followed through and kept her daughter in line. But there was something about her that seemed so familiar. The thought had popped into his head a time or two already that day, and he'd racked his brain to figure out where they'd met.

"That's not what Marcus said," Suzanne called out from behind him, where she now sat beside Luke on the sofa. He turned to see she had her bare feet up on the coffee table.

"What the hell did Marcus say? Marcus, what the fuck did you tell everyone?"

His mom lifted a brow before she walked back into the kitchen, and Suzanne's lips twitched as she lifted the beer to take a swallow. She was always messing with him.

"You talking about your new neighbors?" Marcus appeared, Karen behind him. She was the only one of them to inherit their mom's shortness, standing at barely over five feet, wearing a gray sundress, her hair dyed vibrant red and pulled up into a messy bun.

"Heard she's hot," Suzanne added.

"And heard she comes with a kid who's trouble." Karen pointed her wineglass, likely filled with the same Chablis she always drank, toward Ryan as she sauntered across the living room.

"And he said you knew each other?" Owen strode in from the kitchen, his jeans torn at the knee and faded T-shirt wrinkled.

Their mom reappeared, setting a breadbasket in the middle of the table. She lifted a brow again, and Ryan dragged his gaze back over to Marcus, who was standing there with a big shit-eating grin as he lifted his beer. He really loved stirring things up.

"Is there anything you can keep to yourself?" Ryan snapped.

Marcus just shrugged. "What can I say, Ryan? You seem to attract trouble, drama, and…"

"Difficult women," Luke added, which had everyone looking at him. He was showing the first signs of emerging from his war headspace, which he'd been living in since arriving a few days earlier.

"So where do you know her from?" Karen asked as she perched on the stool of the chair opposite Luke.

Everyone gave him their undivided attention, and he lifted his beer, took a swallow, and breathed out before doing what dickheads did when they didn't want to answer: He shrugged and said, "Can't remember, but when I do, I'll be sure not to tell Marcus."

Chapter 3

Jenny was on her knees in the dirt, pulling out the last of the dried flowers that had died weeks ago, when she spotted Ryan O'Connell pulling into his driveway in a ranger's vehicle emblazoned with the logo of the Montana Department of Fish, Wildlife and Parks.

From what she could see, he hadn't changed one bit. He was still the same tall, broad-shouldered, arrogant asshole she fondly remembered, and she was reeling over the fact that he lived right next door to her! Like, what kind of sick joke was this?

He stepped out of his vehicle in his uniform, and the way he walked with his holstered gun, she couldn't pull her gaze from him. She peered at him from between the rusty Hyundai she was still trying to sell and her newer used little Jeep, and she sat up straighter, remembering that her tank top barely covered her practical bra. She knew the gleaming white showed at the sides, and she pulled at the blue spaghetti strap of her cotton tank to cover herself.

What could she say? Going braless wasn't an option with her generous C cups.

"See you're finally getting around to cleaning up that mess?" he said, looking right at her from over the tops of his mirrored shades. He walked across her driveway and onto her grass as if she'd invited him over.

Even the way he said it had her fighting her first instinct, which was to hit back at him with some cutting remark. Instead, she just fisted her hands as she rested them on her thighs and took in the pile of dead annuals in the dirt. She didn't have a clue what they once had been, considering she didn't have a green thumb on her.

"I guess it's a matter of opinion, really," she said. "Not sure why you're offering yours to me." Ooh, she wanted to pat herself on the back. She sensed that his smile and soft chuckle were not from humor, and he lifted his gaze, taking in everything about her aunt's house.

"I knew the woman who lived here for years. She was a fantastic, generous, sweet lady who knew how to be a neighbor—you know, respectful, courteous. She really took pride in her place. It's gone downhill. Likely a little too much for you to look after?"

Yup, she got the zinger. Apparently he had a cruel streak, too, considering he was commenting on her character. She had to fight the urge to roll her shoulders. This was the kind of judgy shit she hated, and it never got old with assholes who thought they knew her.

"Guess a privileged white boy like you would think that," she snapped. "You see a woman and her daughter alone and they're, what, not capable because neither has a penis?" She took in the shock on his face as he pulled off his shades and tucked them in his shirtfront.

"Uh, no," he said in a low voice, though he didn't have the decency to even look embarrassed at having been called out. In fact, he took a step closer, and she had to tilt her head to look up. "This privileged white boy, as you so aptly put it, lived next door to a single old woman who had one of the nicest yards and gardens in the area. She made everything about it look easy. And I was raised by a single mom of six who worked harder than three white men put together and never asked for help. Just stating what I see."

Nothing like having him point out that she was the one who'd just jammed her foot in her mouth. She could feel her face heat, and she had to pull in a breath and try to regain what she could of her dignity before she came out looking like a bigger idiot. She pressed her tongue against her top teeth as she stared up at Ryan, whose eyes were bluer than she remembered. Perpetual tan, good looks. She had to pull it together.

"Well, this has been fun," she said. "Are you done pointing out my shortcomings, or maybe you have a few more digs you'd like to add?"

He didn't smile this time, but his gaze seemed intense, hard. "So you bought this and moved in a few weeks ago. Just you and your daughter live here? You didn't say last night if there was a husband, boyfriend, significant other in the picture or any other kids."

She hadn't bought the house, but she wasn't about to share that with Ryan. "As I said, it's just me and my daughter." Something about kneeling in front of a man didn't work for her, so she brushed her hands together to wipe off some non-existent dirt, pressed them to the grass, scooted her feet around, and stood up.

Ryan didn't even step back. Just the scent of him made her angry, because it was too appealing. She let her arms hang to her sides even when he allowed his gaze to skim over her. It was intimate and egotistical and indecent, as if he thought looking at her was his God-given right. His arms were crossed over that amazing chest, which she'd felt skin to skin just one time.

"Your daughter…" he started, and she knew he was waiting for her to step in.

"You mean Alison? Yes, my daughter." She fisted her hands again and could feel her nails digging into her palms.

This time, he did smile, and he pulled his gaze over to the house. She couldn't shake the feeling that he was interrogating her. "Yeah, Alison. You have a talk with her about the noise? It's been going on every night since you moved here. I'm assuming you're not home at night? She's like, what, sixteen, seventeen…"

Oh, here we go. The topic of Alison wasn't open for discussion. "She's almost fifteen, and I work afternoons, evenings. Again, I told you the noise won't happen anymore. I know about it now, and I put my foot down."

Actually, her daughter was fourteen and three months, nowhere close to being fifteen. Regarding the stereo, Jenny had yanked the audio connection from the speaker and hid it in her underwear drawer, because her daughter hadn't been known for her compliance as of late, as illustrated by the nose ring two weeks earlier and the jet-black hair the previous week.

"Where do you work?" Ryan asked. Boy, she was really getting the sense of a full-out interrogation.

"Mini-mart," she said. Counting cash in the back room and reconciling statements for the small grocery store was the only job she was qualified for, considering her late husband had been the sole breadwinner—his insistence and her mistake.

"So you work for Joel."

What was it about the way Ryan spoke? She wondered what he was holding back. She had to fight the urge to lean in or yell and ask him what the fuck he wanted with her, to stop toying with her.

"Yes, so if that's all…" she started before those blue eyes zeroed in on her again.

"Can't figure out where we met. I'm pretty good with faces, and you didn't answer me last night."

She didn't want to answer him now, either, but he showed no intention of leaving. Maybe his stubborn streak had been what attracted her, the idea of a strong-minded male. She had to force the image of him and that night she'd never forget, being underneath him, from her mind.

"Well, this is kind of embarrassing," she said. "You picked me up at the Lighthouse Bar, took me home with you, and screwed my brains out. Apparently, I wasn't that memorable. Not sure how to take that."

There it was: the first time she'd seen him rattled. She would've taken some enjoyment from it if her ego hadn't taken such a shit-kicking at the thought of being so forgettable.

Then she heard a beep. The smoke alarm—hers. Dammit, Alison! What the hell had she gone and done now?

Chapter 4

Very few people had the ability to shock Ryan anymore, as he would've sworn he'd seen and heard just about everything. Except now, as Jenny raced into the house, all he could do was stand there and stare, trying to picture her and place her face from his memory of a night so long ago.

She had basically called him out as a despicable bad boy. Jenny was slim and curvy, with long legs, a generous bust under her faded tank top, and a great ass, from what he could see by the sway of it under her short shorts. She was not someone he'd easily forget, and he was stuck on the Lighthouse Bar.

Like, what the fuck? It wasn't as if Ryan was a boy scout, but at the same time… It was in that second that the familiarity about his new neighbor, which he hadn't been able to put his finger on, hit home—the where, when, and how.

It had been a long time ago, before he was a ranger.

He pulled his hand over his jaw, barely hearing the

scrape of whiskers over the constant sharp beeping of the smoke detector from inside the house.

He could hear voices, shouting, and something of the discord between mother and daughter as he found himself walking up the steps and taking in the open screen door, assessing everything. Through the smoke, he could see the girl. What the hell was her name? Right, Alison. And then there was Jenny, who was standing now on a stool that appeared to have seen better days, reaching for the smoke detector.

"Is there a fire?" he called out, his cell phone already in his hand, just as the beeping stopped.

"Just my daughter," Jenny snapped, holding the detector battery.

He automatically held out his hand to take the battery and help her down, and she hesitated only a second before accepting it. The teen who seemed to be the source of every problem was swatting the smoke that billowed from the stove. There was just something about her that he recognized. She was badass, looking for trouble, with a major chip on her shoulder.

"I told you to dump that pan in the sink! Why weren't you watching it…?" Jenny yelled as she strode back into the kitchen.

With a better view now, Ryan didn't miss the fact that Alison's jet-black hair was spiked and suddenly short. What had she done, hacked it off with scissors? It appeared that way, considering the mess it was in. As he moved closer, he could see through the smoke that she wore a nose ring and heavy eye makeup, and her shorts were absolutely inde-cent. The tank she wore was loose and backless. She wasn't saying anything as Jenny took the fry pan, flames still flick-ering inside, and dumped it in the sink. Smoke billowed again, but the smoke detector was now disabled.

He rested the battery on the island, which was covered in cans, boxes, and packaging, and then walked over to the back door to pull it open to let some of the smoke out.

"Seriously, Alison, what is this now, the silent treatment?" Jenny said. "You're not two years old. You could have burned the house down. How many times have I told you that you don't put something on the stove and walk away and leave it unattended? You know better. You're supposed to be responsible, yet all you've done since we've moved here is cause trouble. Whenever something happens, all I can think is 'What have you gone and done now?'"

Of course, what did Alison do but roll her eyes? He sensed that she was about to dish out some attitude, but she didn't have to say a word. She crossed her arms over her chest, her body too much like a grown woman's for a girl who was all about trouble.

"You're the one who insisted on moving here without giving me a choice," Alison said. "I had a life in Atlanta. My friends were there. You completely destroyed my life, so I'd say you're getting exactly what you deserve. You screwed with my social life and basically said to hell with me. It was all about what you wanted…"

"Oh, stop it, already," Jenny said. "You know we had to leave. I had no choices, Alison. We had no choice, so instead of causing problems, how about you be part of the solution and try to make the best of it?"

"Blah blah blah, same old—"

"Hey, don't talk to your mother like that," Ryan snapped, cutting off the teenage attitude and the back-and-forth between mom and daughter, which seemed to be spiralling downward into a battle of wills that wouldn't go anywhere.

Both Jenny and Alison stared at him in that minute,

maybe from shock or surprise or something. He walked back into the center of the kitchen and stood there, feeling very much like a referee.

"What the fuck is he doing in here?" Alison jabbed her finger his way.

The smoke wasn't as thick now with the doors open, front and back, but his eyes were still burning. He gave everything to the kid. How old was she, fifteen going on trouble? She had a smart mouth on her, and he didn't miss the annoyance in Jenny's tone when she replied.

"Ryan was outside," she said. "We were talking when you set the smoke detector off. And watch your mouth, Alison—and, while we're at it, clean up this mess you made. We need to talk about a few things, establish some ground rules."

He understood the way Jenny snapped at her daughter, but at the same time, he could see it wasn't accomplishing anything. The girl just wasn't reasonable.

Ryan sensed a lot of unresolved issues between the two of them, but now he had an answer to at least one of his questions. So she had moved from Atlanta. He took in the mess of the kitchen, the dirty dishes, the packaging and open cans and boxes stacked on the table and floor. Still moving in, it appeared.

Jenny was walking his way, pulling at the spaghetti strap of her tank, which didn't cover her wide bra strap. There was something about the motion that made him unable to pull his eyes from her bust. He dragged his gaze up to her face, round, cute, with eyes the color of taffy. Her body too was unforgettable, and she tried to wrap her arms around herself as if she was uncomfortable, but all it did was accentuate the size of her breasts. He realized he was staring, and he had to force himself to look at her face again. Was that how he had acted the night he'd met her?

"See anything you like?" she said, and he didn't think she was happy.

He didn't say anything. He knew he should be embarrassed, but there was something about her. He wasn't sure what to make of her demeanor, her sass, her attitude. His memories of her didn't seem to fit the woman who was standing before him now, unsmiling.

"I told you I was good with faces," he said. "So, the Lighthouse Bar... How many years ago was it, Jenny, or Jennifer, or Jenn? I suppose this should make things awkward. So you came from Atlanta, just you and your daughter, why?" He crossed his arms over his chest, staring down at her, and he wasn't sure what to make of her expression.

She made a rude noise and stepped closer to him before glancing over her shoulder to Alison, who appeared to be listening to everything. Then she rested her hand on his arm. Her touch was soft, her fingers slender. "It's Jenny, just Jenny. Can I talk to you outside, please?" she said, her voice low.

He suspected her pissed-off tone was from the round with her daughter, but at least now he knew what he'd done to set her on edge. He found himself following her outside after taking a last look at Alison in the kitchen. She was the kind of kid he'd come across one too many times, looking for trouble and landing in it.

Jenny made a point of closing the door and rested her hand on her hip, looking down at the gray porch. He could see she was thinking of something to say, and from how on edge she was, he didn't think it was polite conversation she had in mind.

She lifted her gaze to him again. "If you don't mind, I'd rather not have my daughter knowing about us and what happened. It was years ago, and as you can see, it's the kind of thing she'd hold over me. Besides, it was a long time ago, so how about we skip going down memory lane? I'd say it's great to see you, but it isn't, really, because apparently I'm so unmemorable that you didn't even remember me. And you know what? It's fine. I don't need you to remember me. Actually, I'd prefer it, and you have my permission to ignore me completely over here. Don't be neighborly, don't come over, don't even say hi. You mind your business, and I'll mind mine…" She gestured to him with the flat of her hand, a motion to leave. When he didn't move, she strode down the steps ahead of him, making another rude noise.

Ryan took his time on the stairs, walking down, trying to figure out why she was so angry. "You don't know what I'm thinking or what I remember, so don't put words in my mouth," he said. "You said you just moved back here from Atlanta? Guess that would explain a lot, but at the same time, I'm having trouble understanding your attitude toward me." He was wondering what was different about her, too.

She stood for a second in shock, and her entire body seemed to still. "You don't understand my attitude toward a man who's the love 'em and leave 'em kind of guy? You picked me up, slept with me, and…"

"Get your story straight." He cut her off. "Seems there were two of us involved, and you're the one who walked over to me in that bar. You were offering, and you bet I took you up on it. At the same time, where were you when I woke up?"

Her eyes widened. It was always the same when he called someone out. Her breath squeaked, her face flushed, and she said nothing.

"Gone is where you were," he said. "I reached over in

my bed, expecting warm skin, a warm body, but instead I touched cool sheets. If you really want to do the finger-pointing thing, it was you, Jenny, who ran out on me."

Chapter 5

"I've left several messages for you, and you haven't called back. As I said in every one of my messages, this can't wait. This is a matter of urgency. The situation is becoming untenable with your daughter, and I must speak with you and your husband."

Jenny had her cell phone pressed to her ear, still feeling the knot in her stomach after seeing the name of Alison's school on her cell phone and knowing they wouldn't call unless there was a problem.

She pulled open the bottom drawer of her steel desk and lifted out her purse. She was in a jean skirt, and her legs were bare, her shoes flat and practical. "I'm sorry. You said this is…"

"Mrs. Kramer, the principal at the high school."

Right. She pressed her hand to her forehead. Just on the other side of the door, her boss was talking with some customers. She hoped he'd stay out there and leave her in the now empty office, as it made it easier to talk.

"I see," she said. "I didn't get a message, I'm sorry. You called my cell phone, not my home?"

"I called your home, several times. Left messages for both you and your husband."

She pulled the phone away, hearing the woman still talking, and silently cursed her daughter under her breath, calling her every name she could think of and wanting to put her hands on her and shake her. Of course, Alison had probably deleted the messages. Who else had called? There was also the fact that the principal was asking about her husband.

She put the phone back to her ear. "I'm sorry, Mrs. Kramer, but I didn't get a message. If I did, I'd have called you. I'm just at work right now, but…"

"I'm sorry to call you there, but this is a situation that can't wait. I need to meet with you now." There was something about the way she spoke, the demand, that didn't quite sit right. Jenny sensed the principal's annoyance loud and clear. That was just something her daughter was gifted at, pushing everyone's buttons, especially hers.

She stood up, seeing the time on the big round analog clock, eleven thirty. It was close enough to lunch. "Well, I'm at work, as I said, but I'm about to step out for lunch. I could stop by." She looked at the door again and spotted her boss, Joel, who was ten years her junior, coming her way. He was balding, with a beard, a little on the heavy side. She put everything into the call now, determined to get off the phone before he walked back in. Family problems and unruly teenagers were exactly what she couldn't bring into work if she wanted to keep her job.

"So you're on your way, then." The principal had a way of talking that made Jenny feel herself beginning to sweat. She was unable to shake the idea that she'd just been called in to the principal's office.

"Yes, I'll be there in fifteen minutes," she said, then hung up just as the door opened and Joel strode in. He gave everything to her in a look. At times, she didn't know what to make of him and couldn't tell what he thought of her.

"I'm going to take off for lunch, if that's okay?" she said and dumped her phone in her purse, then rested it on the desk, which was neat and tidy. Standing there waiting for the man to tell her it was okay was humbling, just another reason her job was nothing more than a job. Money didn't grow on trees, so there she was.

"You get the statement of reconciliation over to Clive, and the overages?" Joel said. Right, he was still second-guessing everything she did. He looked hard at her, or rather at her breasts.

"An hour ago," she said.

Then he was at his desk against the other wall, lifting papers and giving everything to them. For a second, she didn't think he would answer about lunch, and she pulled in a breath and waited.

He finally lifted his gaze after what felt like minutes but she knew had been only a few seconds, as if he'd decided what she could do. That was something she hated, being treated like a child.

"Sure, just make sure you punch out, as well," he said.

That was another reason why Joel was the boss of this chain, because he was even better at pinching pennies for the corporation than she suspected the CEOs were themselves. God forbid they had to pay an employee an extra five dollars, but she forced a smile to her face, taking in his frown.

"Absolutely," she said, although she wondered at times whether he even went through the timecards to make sure everyone had actually punched out.

It took her nine minutes to drive to the school, and she pulled into the student parking lot because there wasn't a spot left in the staff parking. She stepped out, feeling the angst, and pulled out her cell phone as she took in the teens leaning against an old Plymouth. She locked the door of the Jeep, then pulled up her daughter's name and sent off a quick text.

Are you in class?

Three dots appeared. *Why?*

She rolled her shoulders. Alison knew every one of her buttons to push, including how to not answer a question.

Your principal called. She started walking around the kids and into the school, waiting for her daughter to respond.

She could see the three dots as if Alison was thinking of what to say, but then there was nothing.

No idea why she'd call me? Jenny wrote. Two could play that game.

Three dots appeared again. *What did she say?*

She had to fight the urge to roll her eyes as she pulled open the school door, not expecting to have to come back only a few weeks after registering her daughter for the start of the year in August.

Well, why don't you tell me? I've been called in to the office because of a problem with you—by your principal!

There was nothing, no dots.

"Little shit," she muttered under her breath, seeing her daughter was now giving her the silent treatment. Great, just great. She was walking into the lion's den, so to speak, and she didn't have a clue what her daughter had done.

She spotted the door to the office and pulled it open before stepping in and seeing four women at desks behind the counter, each with a computer in front of her. No one was looking her way as she stood there waiting. She took in her cell phone and didn't miss the lack of response from her daughter still, but she tucked it into her purse.

She looked at the big clock on the wall and knew she

had to be back to work in half an hour, so she finally cleared her throat, but no one looked up. Geez, uncomfortable. It reminded her so much of when she'd gone to school.

"Um, excuse me…" She tapped her fingers on the counter, as well.

"Just a minute, please," a gray-haired woman said without looking up. It seemed it was another minute before she looked her way. "Yes, can I help you?"

"I'm here to see the principal, Mrs. Kramer. She's expecting me."

The woman stood up. She wore polyester knit slacks and a navy shirt that wasn't all that flattering, and her hair looked like it needed some work. "Can I tell her your name?

"Yes, Jenny Sweetgrass," she replied, having to fight the urge to say more.

"Just have a seat," the woman said.

Jenny stepped away from the counter, seeing the cheap padded chairs, and opted to stand. She wanted to get in and get out. She reached for her phone again, hoping her daughter had replied, but she took in the blank screen and knew that would have been too easy. When she looked up, a tall woman with light hair and a navy jacket, a little on the heavy side, was striding up to the counter.

"Jenny, I'm Helen Kramer," she said. "Thanks for coming right down. Come in. Let's talk in my office."

She followed Mrs. Kramer around the counter and down a hall, then into an office at the end. The woman had to be close to six feet tall and was likely two hundred pounds. As Mrs. Kramer sat down behind the desk, Jenny also took a seat and spotted a file in front of her with her daughter's name printed along the top. Great! She wondered what notes they were keeping on her. Judging by the volume of pages, a lot.

"First, I just want to remind you that we haven't received your daughter's transcripts from the school in Atlanta," Mrs. Kramer said. "These are records we need…"

"I'm sorry. I'll call them again and find out what's taking them so long, but when you called, you said there was a problem with my daughter. I do have to be back to work soon, so I'll need to leave," she said, not missing the annoyance on the principal's face.

"Well then, I'll get right to it. Your daughter is a troublemaker. She's been kicked out of physics class and hasn't turned in one assignment, and of the twenty-four days she's been enrolled at this school, she's missed nineteen— all parent excused." Mrs. Kramer was looking at the file and then flicked her blue eyes Jenny's way.

Her teeth were clenched so hard that her jaw ached, because she realized it was sarcasm in the principal's tone. "Parent excused?" she said, wondering whether that was her voice that had squeaked. How many parents had sat right where she was and had to listen to this principal tell them how rotten their kids were? With Alison, she knew without a doubt it was true.

"Yes, it appears your husband has excused her," Mrs. Kramer said. "We have guitar lessons three times, sick with the flu four times, a grandmother in the hospital, a holiday, and…"

She wondered if she had stopped breathing as she stared at the woman, who was now returning her stare.

"So, as I said when I called you, I left you several messages, and here we are. Imagine my surprise when I pulled her records and saw that the registration you filled out has only your contact information, not your husband's.

There's no information about her father, so of course, given all the absences, I have to ask…"

Mrs. Kramer was leaning over her desk and pulled her pen out, clicking it over and over expectantly, ready to write.

All Jenny could think was to wonder what her daughter was thinking. She wanted to wring Alison's neck. At the same time, she wasn't about to come clean to the principal about her life or her daughter's, because personal was personal. That was just not something she was about to do.

"The absences? This is the first I'm hearing about it, and I can assure you her father didn't take her out of school…" She lifted her hands in the air and then let them fall on the purse resting on her lap. Seeing the expression on the principal's face, the open question, her mind was now spinning on how to answer, so she finally said, "Because her father is dead."

Chapter 6

Ryan loved everything about Livingston, how it was nestled under the big sky in one of the most beautiful parts of the world, in Paradise Valley, surrounded by the Absaroka Range in the east and the Gallatin Range to the west, next to the Yellowstone River, with the best fishing. He didn't want his little piece of the world featured on the front page of any travel magazines, as that would only attract the crazies. Putting it on the roadmap meant it would be flooded by tourists every year. No, he loved the balance there and the fact that the crime rate didn't compare to the average in the rest of the country.

Being under the radar was often a good place to be, in his humble opinion. He couldn't imagine living anywhere else—but he hadn't been able to get his rather prickly neighbor, Jenny, who seemed to be steeped in mystery, from his mind.

What did he know about her, really? How many years had it been since he'd picked her up and slept with her? That night of sex was as vivid in his memory as if it had happened that very day. How had he not placed her the minute he saw her?

Everything about her left him with the feeling that something about her didn't add up, but at the same time, he had to remind himself she was just a neighbor, and she wasn't his business. Curiosity about her was a one-way ticket to a problem he didn't need or want.

He took in the streets and the people as he drove in his pickup. When he spotted his brother Marcus driving the opposite way toward him in his cruiser, he lifted his hand in a wave as he passed. Just two brothers who had raised hell in this town and were now running it, his brother the cop, him the ranger. Both were the law around here, on and off the streets. At one time, they had been young hooligans, out of hand, thinking they were outsmarting everyone. That was likely why he was as good at sniffing out trouble as he was now.

He wasn't sure what made him look, but over on the sidewalk by the high school was the source of his distraction, Jenny. Her dark hair was hanging loose, and she was dressed casually in a short jean skirt. She seemed agitated, with her cell phone to her ear, talking.

He knew he should keep driving, but he just couldn't help himself: He jerked the wheel, pulled over fast, and stopped, then shoved his truck in park at the curb and took in the shock on her face as she pulled the phone away from her ear. He stepped out of the truck and walked around, realizing an instant too late how this might look.

"Everything okay?" he said. He wondered what his brother would say if he knew what he'd done.

"Fine. Why…why did you pull over?"

It was just something in her voice, but he sensed she was pissed off, upset, and something else. At him? Maybe. She gestured toward his truck, and he took in the cell phone she was still holding. He didn't bother to pull his shades off in the bright Montana sun. Just something about wearing them made him feel like he could sense so much more about a person, because they couldn't really tell where he was looking. It also created a sense of uneasiness that he liked.

"Saw you, is all," he said. "You looked a little on edge, upset, and I wasn't happy about how we left things yesterday."

Namely, he wasn't happy about how she seemed to think he'd left her when it had been the other way around. Her message had been loud and clear, sneaking out while he was asleep without even a Dear John. Had he wanted to see her again? Then, absolutely.

She lifted her hand, and for a second, he wasn't sure what she was going to say. He took in the school behind her and the kids out front. Some of them he knew, either from their parents or from something they'd done, but many he didn't.

"You know, I don't really have time for this right now, or for you," she said. "I thought I was pretty clear. You don't need to be friendly, and I think you made a point of setting me straight. Fine, I get it. Right now, I have more important things…"

Her cell phone was ringing, and he didn't miss the name of the mini market that flashed on the screen before she answered. He was pretty sure she swore under her breath before putting the phone to her ear.

"Hey, Joel. Yeah, I know I'm late and was supposed to be back at work, but I've kind of run into a little problem with my daughter, and I can't make it back…" Her hand was over the back of her neck, and she turned and gave him her back. She was on edge. He didn't have a clue what Joel was saying to her on the other end, but he made no move to get back in his truck, which he now could see was parked at an odd angle.

"Yes, yes, I know, but I'll definitely make up the hours…"

Okay, so her boss was giving her the gears. He could do the decent thing and walk away, but he knew Joel could be kind of a prick at times, not the easiest guy to work for. He'd always been out to prove something to everyone.

"Sure, dock me, fine…" She slapped the side of her leg, then ran her hand over her forehead to brush back her hair. He could see how agitated she was. "Fine, fine," was all she said, then hung up and let out a sigh.

He was pretty sure Joel had hung up on her first, by the way she pulled the phone away from her ear.

"Look, I seriously don't have any patience left, Ryan, so if you don't mind, I have a daughter I need to track down. I don't want to have to answer to any more questions or explain myself or be accountable to one more person—"

"Your daughter's missing?" he said. He took in the kids and wondered what Alison had done now. There was just something about her that reminded him so much of that song "Bad to the Bone." She was on a one-way road to finding herself in cuffs, in front of a judge, with a record, or worse.

Jenny groaned and squeezed her phone. "Oh, I'd say she's ignoring me, not answering my texts. I just got called in to the principal's office only to find out that she's missed most days of school so far this year, and this is the first I'm hearing of it. Guess she thinks not answering me and ignoring me is the way to handle it. Now my boss is pissed at me, and my job, which I hate anyway, is basically hanging by a thread. Even the principal is questioning everything about me, and now I have to deal with the likes of you? Seriously, Ryan, I have no time, so…"

He reached over and rested his hand on her arm. "Hey, just take a breath. I'm not your enemy here. So when was the last time you talked to her?"

She said nothing for a second and just stared at him, then blinked. There was something about her eyes, deep brown, and he was pretty sure it was those eyes that had hooked him before. They were unforgettable. She lifted her hand again and let it fall to her side.

"Oh, about an hour ago, as I was pulling up to the school, I texted her and asked her where she was. When I said I was at the school, she went silent. You know how teenagers can be a pain in the ass, but Alison is just…" She didn't say anything else.

He could sense that the teen was the source of many sleepless nights, angst, and a ton of stress. Alison was just the kind of kid who could make people decide that having kids was not something they ever wanted to do.

"Difficult, I can see," he said. "A truant, for sure. Have you tried tracking her? Do you have that app?" He took in her confusion and pulled out his phone. "Give me her cell phone number and I'll see where she is."

It was another second before she shrugged and rattled off the number.

He sent off a quick text to Marcus: *Check this cell phone and tell me where it is.*

He waited a second. Three dots appeared. *Why?*

Just do it.

Give me a minute. Just pulling into the office.

"So what are you doing?" Jenny asked, and he glanced over the rim of his shades at her. The questions in his mind about her just seemed to be piling up. So she had been in Atlanta. For how long? Why had she disappeared the night she'd slipped from his bed? She had a husband, a daughter, a family, but how had she come to live right next door to him? When would be a good time to find out? Was she divorced, still married, or what? Maybe after they tracked her daughter down, he'd take some time to cut right to it and get some of the answers he seemed to think he needed.

"Finding out where your daughter is," he replied. "It'll take a minute. So is this something she does often?"

Jenny glanced away, and he sensed she was pissed off and had likely taken the question personally or something. There was just something about her, the emotion, the personality, but he sensed there was more about this woman. He shouldn't want to know, but he just couldn't help himself.

"So you automatically assume that my daughter is a problem, like she does this all the time? You probably think she's irresponsible, walking trouble, and I must be a bad parent for having a kid who acts out this way."

He just stared at her, taking in his phone and the lack of response from his brother. He'd said a minute, and evidently he'd meant it. "Don't put words in my mouth. I'm having a little trouble with the leap you've made. I guarantee you have no idea what I'm thinking. It's called getting answers. I don't know your daughter or why she does what she does, but I do know what I see. She's angry and acting out. You've texted or called her, but she hasn't answered you."

Everything about Jenny and the way she stood, the way she breathed, told him how agitated she was. It was something no one could hide, not from him.

"I texted dozens of times," she said. "She doesn't answer the phone, ever, so I know leaving a voicemail is pointless. As I said, when she doesn't want to answer me, I get silence." She held up her phone as if making a point.

He knew when a kid was hiding something and didn't

want to face consequences. "You're sure she's not at school?"

The look she gave him said everything. "Unless she's hiding in some corner, she's not here. Her teachers all marked her absent." She pulled in another breath and lifted her hands, then let them fall. "She hates school. She basically hates everything and everyone right now. So no, I guarantee you she's not here."

Okay, point made. He found himself lifting his gaze, taking in the grounds, the street, the cars. "Chances are she'll be at home. You could go home and wait for her," he suggested. Just then, there was a ding on his phone, and he took in the text from his brother.

Livingston Peak, halfway to the summit. Here's the link. Isn't this your neighbor's daughter, Alison Sweetgrass? Something I need to know? WTF is she doing in the park? Evidently on an afternoon hike!

He just stared at the text and could feel without having to look up that Jenny was staring at him. "Found her," he said, then sent off a quick reply to his brother. *Thx! Not yet. Will get back to you.*

"Where?" she said.

He glanced up as he clicked the link to see her location, knowing exactly where that was. What the hell was Alison thinking? "On a hiking trail, in the middle of nowhere, so I guess that answers one of my questions. Your daughter apparently decided to go for a hike up Livingston Peak instead of going to school."

She was a kid with a chip on her shoulder and was likely looking for trouble. She hadn't seemed like the type who'd take a hike to figure things out, but maybe he was wrong.

"So we have two options here," he continued. "You go home and wait for her to show up, or we go into the park after her."

She set her jaw. Yeah, Alison was on exactly the wrong side of her pissed-off mom. "We? You said 'we.'"

He wasn't sure what to make of the way she said it, so he shrugged. "You seem to forget what I do. This is my area, my park. Not much goes on that I don't know about, and I'm certainly not sending you off alone when I'm the one who knows where she is. My advice is for you to go home and wait. She'll show up eventually."

And meanwhile, he would absolutely drive out and see what Alison Sweetgrass was up to in his park. There was just something about the girl that was so rough around the edges, and he'd bet his bottom dollar that she was making the worst choices possible. That was not the kind of careless troublemaker he wanted running around in his park.

Jenny was already shaking her head. "No, I'm not going home. Like, what the hell would she be doing on the trail?"

"Going for a hike," he said.

The face Jenny made said everything. "Not likely."

Yeah, he thought as much, considering kids who looked and acted like Alison didn't often go for the scenery or a quiet stroll in nature. Alison was the kind of girl who had no idea what she was getting herself into. There were bears and cougars, and he was sure she didn't have any idea of the other dangers out there. Some kids did, but not Alison, for sure.

"You sure you want to go up after her?" was all he asked.

Jenny gave everything to him in her glare. She was pissed, angry. "My daughter, my problem. I don't plan on waiting hours until she decides to show up. I've had about enough of her crap."

He just shrugged, picturing the confrontation that was

likely to happen when they tracked her down. "Fine, let's go," he said and took in the surprise on her face.

"You mean with you?"

He started to the passenger door of his truck and pulled it open. "If you want to find your daughter in my park, then yeah, you bet it's with me. I'm the only one who can use the back road up. There's no public access." He took in her hesitation and something else in her expression, and then what did she do but lift her chin, tuck her purse over her shoulder, and climb into the passenger side of his truck?

He just stood there for a second. She wouldn't look his way, uncomfortable, and he couldn't shake the feeling that there was so much about her that he might not want to know. Was she hiding something? Definitely.

He gave the door a shove and started around to the driver's side, stuck on the fact that both mother and daughter were steeped in something that didn't quite sit right with him. If he was smart, he'd help her find her daughter and then listen to his brother and keep his distance.

But then, Ryan had never been that smart when it came to women.

Chapter 7

here are you? Why are you on a hiking trail at Livingston Peak?

She wrote the text to her daughter from where she sat in the passenger side of Ryan's truck. She'd never expected to see him again. At the same time, there was something about her life. She'd moved herself and her daughter from Atlanta for a fresh start because her aunt had died and left Jenny her house, a surprise she was still wrapping her head around—except this fresh start seemed to be turning into just a different version of the trouble she'd walked away from.

"You texting her again?"

She hesitated before looking over to Ryan. Being in his proximity was doing things to her reasoning that she didn't like. She'd put him from her mind years ago, told herself he was the bad boy she'd picked up in a bar for a night of sex, and he'd never amount to anything. She was having a lot of trouble with the fact that she was now sitting in his truck while he drove her into the park where her daughter supposedly was. She couldn't keep her head screwed on straight. "I am," she said.

"Don't," he replied as her thumb hovered over the green send button.

"Why not?"

A smile or something pulled at the edges of his mouth, and he shook his head. "Because the minute you do, she's on to you. Right now, we have the element of surprise on our side. I know where she is, and she doesn't know we're coming. She's ignored every one of the how many texts you've already sent. One more isn't going to have her responding, but it will have her running if she's trying to hide from you, and it seems that's exactly what she's doing."

Why did it seem Ryan O'Connell knew more about her daughter than she did? That didn't sit right with her. "She's my daughter, you know," she said. She couldn't help herself.

"She is, but at the same time, I know kids like her."

What the hell was that supposed to mean? She turned and really looked at him, feeling the slight against her. "Seriously…?" she started before he cut her off.

"Oh, don't go jumping down my throat again. I deal with kids looking for trouble on a daily basis, and I can tell you I used to be one. She's angry, got a chip on her shoulder, acting out, and she's trying to push every one of your buttons. You busted her for something, and she knows she's in a ton of shit, so instead of facing the music, she's avoiding you. Just something kids do, and reasoning skills are definitely not something teens are known for."

She just stared at him, still holding her phone and seeing the text she hadn't sent. She turned off the screen. "So are you a shrink now, too?" she said, knowing it had come out a lot more sharply than she'd planned.

"Got nothing to do with being a shrink, Jenny. I see this all the time. I deal with that part of human nature that goes looking for trouble. And I'm not you, so I'm a hell of a lot more objective."

"Excuse me?" Even she could hear the incredulity in her voice. "What does this have to do with you not being me? I'm her mother. I know her better than anyone." Her heart was hammering, and she had to still her mind and the panic that had her heart pounding and her hands sweating. Did he have any idea of all her secrets? But that was impossible. Only one man ever had.

Wren.

"That's the problem. You're too close to her. You're not seeing it. She's pushing your buttons, Jenny, and she knows just what to say and what to do to get a reaction from you. Not a great or healthy reaction, but she's a teenager. There's a stage where kids who were once reasonable suddenly go brain dead and do things you'd swear they wouldn't do. It's called hormones, and then if you add in something at home, problems, changes, stress, moving, you get a kid acting out. You moved from Atlanta. Where's her father, still there?"

There were the questions. She felt the truck slow and took in where he pulled off the road, up a wide grassy trail with tire tracks down the middle, definitely a back road. He was glancing at his phone. He really seemed to have a handle on what he was doing, in charge, caring. It was unsettling. What could she tell him? Nothing.

"Her father died and left me a mountain of debt. We lost everything. Yeah, she's pissed. We had a nice house, a life, but we had to leave. Moved back to Livingston, to the house my aunt left me. What about you? You have to have kids."

"Althea was your aunt?" he said. "I'm sorry to hear about your husband. But no, no kids, not that I know of."

Her stomach pitched, and for a second she wondered if she'd stopped breathing.

"Relax," he said. "You look as if you're about to puke over there. Did I say something I shouldn't have?"

Yeah, he had. "You know, I didn't know my aunt very well," she said. Good save! She could talk about her eccentric aunt, her father's sister, whom she'd seen only a handful of times, before Alison. Then there was Wren Sweetgrass, a man she had loved and married—that is, until he showed her who he really was the day after he put a ring on her finger.

"She was a sweet old lady, a busybody," Ryan said. "Didn't think she had any family."

Okay, her aunt was a safe subject. "Everyone has family, somewhere," she replied. "Just not everyone knows who their family is."

What the hell was she doing? She pulled her gaze from him and looked out the window. The trail he was driving was like a dirt road. She didn't have a clue where they were.

"You know, in my line of work, I ask a lot of personal questions," he said, "and I always know when someone is hiding something. It's something everyone does, and you do it well."

Her heart thudded again. Did her face show anything?

"Your daughter acting out…I take it this is new, all this behavior you're getting. Kind of makes sense, if her father died. Bad times make everyone do things they wouldn't do in their right mind. Add in teenage hormones, and it makes a world of sense now, what I've seen. When did your husband die? Was this recent?"

She felt the tightness in her chest and glanced out the

window into the middle of nowhere. Why would her daughter be all the way out here? "Yes, kind of…but you know what? I'd really like to not talk about him. We're supposed to be looking for my daughter."

"Understood," he said. "Just one thing, Jenny."

Her stomach knotted again as she waited for the other shoe to drop. What could be coming next? He was smooth and far too curious. She gave him everything. What was it about having lived in stress for so long? With what felt like disasters coming at her from around every corner, she couldn't help but be suspicious of everyone.

She said nothing, as she couldn't even force herself to swallow the lump stuck in her throat. She just looked at him, her hand on the seatbelt shoulder strap, squeezing. It was the only thing she could think to hold on to.

"Just breathe, and know that if you want to talk about it, whatever it is that has you freaked out and running, I'm here, and I'll listen," he said. Before she could think of something polite to say, he was pressing the brakes. "Oh, hold up. According to this, she should be just up here, in the clearing."

As Ryan drove incredibly fast into the grassy clearing, her heart thudded. The view was incredible, but she could feel her anger at her daughter returning. She wanted nothing more than to wrap her hands around her throat and shake her, to yell at her.

But she knew that instead, after she got her daughter back home, later that night, she would go into the bathroom and cry into a towel, silent and alone.

"She should be just up here," Ryan said.

All she could see was grass and a view—and something black on the ground. When he drove closer and shoved the truck in park, she saw that it was just a backpack. She looked around, not seeing her daughter anywhere. They were so high up, and she just couldn't see her daughter walking up there.

"Ryan, uh…" she started, but he was already out of the truck, his shades on.

He walked over to the backpack and picked it up, and by the time she had stepped out and walked over to him, he'd unzipped it. She stared in shock as Ryan rummaged through the bag and pulled out a cell phone with a tiny crack at the top of the screen and a pink lipstick cover.

"That's my daughter's phone," she said as she took in Ryan, the backpack, and what looked like miles of nothing. She wasn't sure what to make of his face.

"And her backpack?" he said, looking around.

She shook her head. "I've never seen that backpack before."

Alison had an old blue flowered backpack that she'd insisted on bringing from Atlanta. It was something her father had given her, the only nice thing he'd done for her —though her daughter had never seen it that way.

He only nodded and stepped back. "Alison!" he shouted.

Jenny stood there, looking around, listening, hoping for a response, but she knew it was just as likely her daughter wouldn't answer. "Now what?" she asked after what felt like a minute of just standing and listening.

Ryan shook his head, walked around to the back of the pickup, and dropped the tailgate. He settled the backpack down on it and pulled out his cell phone, then dialed and pressed it to his ear. "Well, first, I'll call my brother, let him know. Then we're going to go through this backpack and see what we can find. But, word of caution, Jenny, sometimes kids hide things you as a parent may not want to know. Why don't you let me look and see what's in here?

Then I'll take you back to your place, where it's just as likely she'll turn up."

She was already shaking her head, taking in his large hands, the shape of his fingers, which were so much like Alison's. "Nope, I can assure you, Ryan, nothing my daughter could possibly do would surprise me," she replied, but even as she said it, she couldn't help but wonder whether that was merely wishful thinking.

Chapter 8

Alison's phone was password protected, and her mom didn't have a clue what the password was. As well, Ryan was stuck on the fact that the backpack had contained only a few granola bars, a worn black hoodie, a pack of stale cigarettes, and class papers with the name Ollie Edwards written along the top, along with three empty energy drink cans, a half-eaten cheese sandwich in a Ziploc bag, and a can of warm soda.

Jenny didn't have a clue who Ollie Edwards was. They hadn't even packed a bottle of water for their hike, it seemed, and why the hell had the backpack just been sitting in the clearing in the middle of nowhere, with Alison's cell phone still inside?

He was positive the girl had heard the truck approaching and had been determined not to answer. *Pain in the ass, troublemaker, irresponsible...* Did she have any idea in that teenage brain of hers that she was only making things worse? Apparently not. He wondered if anyone would be able to get through to her.

"Ryan, I think we should have kept looking," Jenny said

from beside him in the truck. "We should have stayed up there, or at least me. I should have stayed up there. I would have made her come out, or outwaited her."

As he drove down their street toward her house, he spotted his brother Marcus already there, just stepping out of his cruiser, in his uniform and shades. Marcus looked his way as Ryan pulled up and parked behind the cruiser right in front of his place.

"You seriously think you could have made her answer you?" he said. "I guarantee you staying up there would have had the opposite effect. She's avoiding your texts. Her message is loud and clear. You weren't getting anywhere, and she wasn't answering me, either. You think I'd have left you out there, dressed the way you are? You have no supplies, no water, and you'd get lost. Then there would be two of you out there, wandering, and I'd have to bring in a lot more people to find both of you. You want to look, we'll do it smart, with the right supplies, the right shoes and gear. For all we know, she's likely had enough of the trail and is on her way down."

He wanted to find out why Ollie Edwards's backpack was sitting out in the middle of nowhere with Alison's phone. He didn't recognize the boy's name, but something told him that Alison wouldn't have thought through her new friendship too well.

"For all we know," he continued, "she's likely hiding and will show up before dinner. Kids do stupid things, but they generally always come home for food and sleep."

From the stark expression on her face, he wasn't sure Jenny believed him, but he stepped out of the truck anyway and walked over to his brother, who stood waiting for him, arms crossed over his solid chest, working a piece of gum.

"She show up here?" Ryan asked.

Marcus merely glanced to the house and then over to Jenny, gesturing with his chin. "No idea. Just pulled up here, but let's hope she has. Jenny, do you mind going inside and seeing if your daughter's here—or if she's been here, at least?"

Ryan knew his brother wanted a word alone with him.

"Ah, sure…" was all Jenny said, and he watched as she strode across the brownish grass, past a pile of weeds, and onto the porch, where she pulled open the screen and unlocked the door.

When she went inside, he said nothing for a second. Marcus hadn't pulled his gaze from him. It was the kind of look that said everything.

"What the fuck are you doing, Ryan?" Marcus finally said.

There it was. Not what he'd expected, but close.

"Helping my neighbor," he replied, amazed at how it rolled right off his tongue.

Marcus pulled off his shades and looked over to him in the bright sun as if ready to call him out, but he must have decided it would be wasted breath, as instead he groaned and pulled his hand over his face. "Thought you were going to give your neighbor some breathing room, yet here you are, helping her out. The kid, by the way, in case you don't already know, is trouble. Seen it before, and pretty sure getting a search party going is jumping the gun a bit…"

"Look, there's more to the story," Ryan said. "I saw Jenny in town, and she was upset. Seems her daughter's been skipping school, and she only just found out. Then the kid went radio silent. My guess is because she knows she's busted. At the same time, the way those two go at it reminds me of how Karen and Mom used to go for each other's throats. How long did that last, like two years, starting when she was sixteen?"

Marcus winced. "It was six months, when she was fourteen, but it seemed longer. Yeah, I remember that better than you. Luke was the one always having to jump in. Karen had always been Dad's favorite, and she was angry at Mom for Dad leaving. It was unreasonable, stupid. Nearly took the house down."

Right, his dad had been there one day, gone the next. They'd been young. It was just something they still didn't speak of. He still remembered the conversation that had rocked all of them, when their mom had sat them down at the table and said their dad didn't live there anymore. It was just them now, and they had only each other to depend on. Ryan had been angry. They all had, each showing it in different ways.

He gestured to the house, hearing Jenny calling for her daughter inside. "The kid's dad died, Jenny's husband," he said. "They just moved here from Atlanta."

Marcus leveled a hard look his way. "Recently? Guess that would explain a lot. Geez, that's rough, uprooting and moving away from your friends and home, and losing a parent... Don't know a teenager who would handle that well, or an adult, for that matter. Explains the chip on the shoulder. She likely just wants some space, so why not give it?"

He heard the squeak of the screen door and spotted Jenny on the porch.

"She's not here," she called out.

Ryan started walking toward her, his brother falling in behind him. "Has she been here at all?"

Jenny shook her head. "Not that I can see. Everything looks the way it was left this morning."

"You know, I hate to say this," Marcus said, "but

chances are she's just keeping her head down. She knows she's in a ton of trouble and will likely show up in a few hours. She probably decided to take off for an afternoon hike, clear her head, but she'll show up. She's a teenager. As soon as she's hungry and tired and she's had time to cool down, she'll sneak in. Ryan filled me in. Sorry to hear about your loss, your husband. That's tough on kids."

Ryan wasn't sure what to make of her expression. She glanced away. That was definitely not the look of a woman who was grieving.

"So you expect me to just sit here and wait?" she replied. "Her phone was in someone else's backpack, miles down a trail. I guess I disagree. I know my daughter, and her needing space and then deciding to show up because she's hungry is exactly what she wouldn't do. Yeah, she's angry at life, at the world, mostly at me, but I guarantee you Alison wouldn't head off on an afternoon hike. She's a city girl, grew up in Atlanta. The closest she's ever come to nature was hanging out at the downtown park. She's terrified of getting stung by bees, hates bugs and dirt and trees…" She rested her hand on her hips and let out a sigh of frustration.

"What about this Ollie Edwards?" Ryan said. "Marcus, can you find out who that is? Then we could track him down and likely find Alison, too, or least get an idea of where her head is. We'll find anyone who knows them. You know the drill…"

He'd taken photos of everything, the contents of the backpack, and then he'd taken one of the crumpled-up essays with Ollie Edwards's name on it, but he'd put the backpack back where they had found it. If Alison was out there, he didn't want her left with nothing, and the same went for this Ollie. If they were together, they'd likely go back to retrieve it.

He really wanted to have a sit-down with the boy and get him to share what was going on with his neighbor's daughter. He could tell by his brother's expression, even though it showed very little of what he was thinking, that he didn't agree. He wasn't so sure, either, that Alison wasn't just hiding out, but at the same time, he'd seen the way she'd acted. She was wild and out of control. Who knew what kind of trouble she'd managed to get herself into? If she got lost or hurt, it would be his problem.

"I do know the drill, which is why there's no investigation yet. She hadn't been gone even twenty-four hours yet, and school just got out. You've already said she's walking trouble. She's angry, not the ideal level-headed kid, and as you said, she's been skipping school. She knows she's in trouble and is probably just biding her time until she thinks it's safe to come home or until she's driven her mother crazy enough. I think you and I both know that."

Ryan knew Marcus was thinking of their brother Luke, who'd done something not so different, but he hadn't come home for three days. He'd camped out, making it all the way up the Absaroka Range. Their mother had been frantic, but Luke had been fine.

"This is a kid from Atlanta," Ryan said. "I can't explain it, Marcus. Just humor me. It's different." He pulled the folded paper with Ollie's name on it from his back pocket. "At least find out who this is. I could do it, but as you said, the town's yours, and I want to have a word with Jenny." He shrugged.

"Fine, give it to me," Marcus said and ripped the paper from his hand. It was covered with pencil, doodling and notes, he thought. Marcus started down the steps before looking back up to Ryan and then over to Jenny, who, throughout their entire back-and-forth, hadn't pulled her gaze from them.

"I'm not staying," she said. "As you said, I'm not properly dressed or equipped, but I'll change into a pair of sneakers, and then I'm going back up there. Maybe I'll find her making her way down—"

"It would be best, Jenny, if you stayed here," Marcus said. "Officially, there's no investigation, but unofficially, I'll make some calls. Either of you hear from her or she shows up, call me."

Ryan watched his brother climb into his cruiser, then turned back to Jenny, who had her arms crossed, tense and uncomfortable. He had a feeling that was more about him, though, and if her daughter hadn't pulled this Houdini, she'd likely have told him to get off her property.

"What?" she snapped, maybe because of the way he was looking at her.

"I have some questions, Jenny, and while we're waiting, how about you answer them for me?"

There it was, something in her eyes, her face. She'd stopped breathing. Yeah, he knew when someone was hiding something, but the problem was, he didn't have a clue what her secrets had to do with him.

"About Alison?" Her voice squeaked.

"Sure, we'll get to her, but how about we start with all these secrets you have? I can't help wondering how much they have to do with your daughter and this situation. Then let's work our way back to the night you slipped out of my bed and I never saw you again. I don't know what it is about you, but something has me wondering what it is you're hiding. Whether you're running from something or you've done something, I don't know, but what I do know is when someone's evading me, and that's exactly what you're doing. So let's start at the beginning and work our way up to today."

She opened her mouth, but nothing came out, so she

gave her head a shake and pulled open the door, then stepped into the house, leaving him standing outside, alone.

Yup, she was hiding something. Not really his business, but at the same time, he wasn't about to let it go.

Chapter 9

S he was freaking out.

This was something about her that Wren had always hated, her inability to keep a straight face. That was likely why he'd started keeping things from her, the deeds, the loans, the empty bank accounts.

She heard the door and his footsteps as she rinsed off dishes in the sink and loaded them into the dishwasher. If she stayed busy, then she could keep it together. Ryan was just someone from her past. She didn't really know him, and he had nothing to do with her and Alison. She just had to remind herself.

"Why the hell are you acting this way?" he said. "You're literally freaking out. It seems every time I ask you something, I see this fear in your face as if you're afraid of what else I'll ask. It's the kind of expression I see from people who are trying to hide something, but I can't figure out what this big secret is or why it would matter. Does it have something to do with why your daughter is skipping school and avoiding you and is now off on a trail, doing God knows what?"

Ryan was direct, and he moved into the kitchen, filling space in her home in a way she'd never expected a man to do again. He was watching her, and she was having so much trouble keeping herself together. He was doing that cop thing, trying to figure out what she was thinking. She had to look away. She hadn't ever expected to see him again, and she needed a minute to find her daughter and sit her down and set some ironclad ground rules.

"Everyone has secrets, Ryan…and maybe with Alison, this is her way of getting back at me. I don't know what's going on with her or why she's doing what she's doing. I'm doing the best I can."

"I'm sure you are, but you didn't really answer my question. You do that a lot. So why did you leave Atlanta, Jenny? You said you had to, but what exactly does that mean?"

She shut her eyes, seeing the blood on her hands, her husband in the ER, reliving the moment the doctor had told her he was gone.

She turned away, back to the sink, and rinsed out the coffee grounds from the carafe. She took her time turning around, bending over, closing up the dishwasher, until she was forced to face him.

"My husband died," she said. "I told you that already. And my aunt left me this house. You know, you're making me feel like a criminal, the way you keep asking questions about me, my life. I'm not sure what that has to do with my daughter. You know what? I'd like to just find her, and then we can go back to being neighbors from afar."

He wasn't smiling, standing on the other side of the island. She didn't remember his eyes being so blue. His hair was thick, and he was tall, broad shouldered. Nothing about him seemed anything like the clean-cut man she'd been married to. Wren had been tall, dark, and handsome, and so was Ryan, but not as polished.

"How did your husband die?" he said. He wasn't going to leave it alone.

She pulled in a breath. "Gunshot. He bled out. And before you ask me when, it was four months ago. Yes, it shook my daughter up. Of course she's upset that she lost her father."

He nodded. "And you lost your husband."

Right. She had to look away.

"You said he left you a debt, that you lost everything…" He was still fishing, and she leaned against the sink, resting one hand on her hip. Ryan wanted a lot of answers, and he was still standing there. He should have walked out the door and left her. She didn't understand why he was sticking his nose in her business, asking questions about topics she didn't want to talk about. "You're angry at him."

She gave him everything. "Of course I'm angry. He hid things from me. Is that what you want me to say? He showed me that he was a different person than I'd thought he was. Are we better off? Absolutely. Has it scarred my daughter? Without a doubt. Does she know everything about her father and the kind of man he was? No. She blames me." She shrugged.

Wren had shown only one side to Alison. To her, he had been a hero until the night he wasn't. Jenny pulled her hand over her face, feeling her heart pounding and having to force his image from her mind.

"Look, I don't really want to talk about him," she said, "because our life here has nothing to do with him. He's gone, and everything about our life in Atlanta with him is also gone. There's nothing left other than a few boxes of things and an empty bank account. I had no idea there was no money. Everything was leveraged. Those were words I didn't even understand. I can honestly tell you, coming here, it was like a gift had landed in my lap, a house from an aunt I barely knew, and it's mine. For me, it's a fresh start. Anything else?" She could feel her confidence and took in the way he watched her.

"Yeah, just one more," he said. "What happened to you the night you slipped from my bed and left, no note, no nothing?"

Was he serious? Of course he was. She made herself look him in the eye and not pull her gaze away. "You were a one-night stand," she said. "Can you honestly look me in the eye and tell me that night was anything more than it was? You picked me up, I came over, and you took what I was offering. So what? We were both consenting adults. I left before you woke. It had been a slice, but it was time to go. I wasn't a fool, thinking it was anything else. I didn't even know your name, not really."

Then, three weeks later, she'd met Wren, and nine weeks later, she'd found out she was pregnant. Wren had said it was fine. He'd be Alison's father. After all, Ryan O'Connell had been nothing more than a mistake one night. She'd had no intention of ever seeing him again, and she had no intention now of him ever finding out that Alison was his.

Yet here he was in her kitchen, in her house, in her life, and she was feeling guilt over keeping something from him even though he likely wouldn't have wanted to know.

"Well, that's the thing, Jenny. We'll never know, will we?" he said. Then his phone dinged, and he pulled it from his back pocket, giving everything to the screen.

"What is it?" she asked.

He exhaled. "It's Marcus. He's found Ollie Edwards and is talking with him now. I'm going to head over there, have a word with him too."

She was shaking her head. "Well, that's the thing, Ryan. I've had enough of men trying to keep me in the dark, telling me I have my place, thinking I don't need to know about things when I do. I have a mind. I can figure things out myself. You seem to forget this is my daughter, so if anyone is going to be talking with this Ollie Edwards, it's going to be me."

She wasn't sure what he was going to say. Wren would have told her no and left her, and that would've been the end of it. There was something she'd never liked about a man telling her what to do, how to feel, how to think. After a while, she had begun to feel herself drowning.

Ryan walked around the island until he stood right in front of her, looking at her, still trying to figure her out. She wasn't going to go quietly into the night and be a good girl, as Wren had often told her, as men expected her to be.

"Jenny, I'm not keeping you in the dark about anything," he said. "You're misunderstanding. As you've pointed out, how well do we really know each other? So don't automatically jump to conclusions about what I'm doing. I sense there's more going on here, and maybe this has to do with whatever went on between you and your husband."

What was it about him? As he stood there, doing that alpha thing, she wanted to talk to him, to share with him, willing him to maybe reach over and touch her, but that was a mistake, and she was angry with herself for wanting it.

"Listen to me, Jenny. I'm not asking you to stay here for any other reason than for you to be here when your daughter walks through that door, which is more than likely what's going to happen. I also know that with the way you two go at it, maybe you'll need a referee to keep you from really getting into it and saying something to each other that you won't be able to take back."

"Ryan…"

He lifted his hand when she tried to interrupt him. "Let me finish, Jenny. You're right, I don't know you well, or your daughter, but what I do know is what I see here. She's angry, and you're running, hiding. You've both suffered a loss you're trying to make sense of. Don't think I'm in any way trying to tell you what to do. I'm just trying to solve this quickly. I hope you and your daughter can sit down and iron out whatever your issues are. I've seen it before. I've lived it. Saw my mom go through much the same thing. Instead of thinking I'm the bad guy, how about just working with me here?"

She didn't say anything for a second. Instead, she glanced away. When she felt his hand reach over and touch her shoulder, it was exactly what she hadn't wanted him to do, but it was a touch that felt way too good. "Okay, fine," she said and shrugged, and he pulled his hand away. "I'll stay here, but you're wrong, you know."

Ryan rested both his hands on his waist, above his holstered gun. "About what?" he said. The uniform seemed to only add to how good looking he was.

She exhaled. "This isn't about my husband."

He said nothing at first, just stepped back and then pulled in a breath. Then he said, "Okay, call me if you hear from her," and he walked out the door.

What was it with Ryan O'Connell? Why did he insist on being the good guy, helping her out? She couldn't help wondering what her life and her daughter's would've been like if she'd walked away from Wren and found Ryan and told him about Alison.

"Stop it," she said out loud, once again angry, because there was no point in going down that road of what could have been. Her choice had simply turned out to be the wrong one.

Chapter 10

Ollie's house was just outside Livingston, a single-wide mobile that had seen better days. The grass was waist high in some parts, and junk was piled here and there. Ryan took in his brother standing out front with some guy who had light shoulder-length hair and couldn't have been more than fifteen, he thought.

He pulled up beside a rusty red station wagon and stepped out of his pickup, taking in the scrawny kid. He wore a tan sleeveless shirt and baggy blue jeans, both covered in dirt and appearing to have seen better days. The kid appeared uneasy, looking over to him and then back to Marcus, standing at the base of lopsided stairs that seemed ready to collapse.

"I told you I don't know where she is," the boy said. "How many times do you want me to tell you? I don't even know her that well." His voice was high pitched, fast, loud, trying to be convincing.

Ryan didn't need his brother to tell him this was Ollie Edwards, and Marcus only glanced his way as he came up beside the two. The boy was tall and skinny but still at least three inches shorter than he and his brother.

"You find out how he knows her?" he asked.

Marcus had his arms crossed over his chest the way he did when he was questioning someone. "Ollie, this is Ranger O'Connell. He's also looking for Alison. Why don't you tell him what you told me?"

Another thing his brother did was get the suspect to repeat the story, then catch the inconsistencies. It was harder to remember a lie than the truth.

"I met Alison at school," Ollie said. "I'm a senior. We hung out. She's nice, is all, new to the school. She didn't know anyone. But I got kicked out and haven't seen her in over a week. I swear that's the truth."

"How old are you?" Ryan asked.

"Seventeen. Look, that's all I can tell you. I said I didn't know anything…"

"Why did you get kicked out of school?" Marcus said. "It's the beginning of the school year. You haven't really had a chance to screw up yet."

Ollie was shuffling back and forth, fidgeting. "Smoking," he said.

Ryan and Marcus looked at each other, knowing it would've been more than that, considering they'd both tried smoking in high school. Marcus had been busted by his math teacher and received a slap on the wrist, detention, with the punishment of having to write a five-thousand-word essay on smoking and its dangerous health effects. Ryan had been lucky, having learned from his brother's mistake. He knew that alone wouldn't have been enough to get Ollie kicked out.

"You know, Ollie, I don't like it when I'm lied to," Marcus said, "and not telling me everything is the same as lying. Come on, out with it. I can just as easily put a call in to the principal and find out in two seconds, or you can come clean and start telling me everything."

"Fine," he said. "Look, what does me getting kicked out of school have to do with Alison?" Ollie wrapped his arms over his chest. He was shaking. Yeah, he was scared shitless, and Ryan would've bet anything he knew something or had done something. Whether that had anything to do with Alison, he'd yet to hear.

"Well, why don't you start with telling us why your backpack was found up on the trail at Livingston Peak with your stuff in it, papers from school, among other things?" Ryan said. "You want to talk about that?"

Marcus pulled out the school paper he'd given him earlier and unfolded it, then held it out to Ollie.

"Shit!" Ollie said. "Look, yeah, this is mine, but it was in a backpack I don't have anymore. When I got kicked out of school, Alison was there outside. I was pissed, and I gave it to her. She was always carrying this ratty blue thing. I asked her if she wanted mine, and she said sure and took it. I gave it to her with my things in it and all. I wasn't going to need it anymore. If she hadn't taken it, I would've dumped it in the trash. I've got a job now, working with my dad as a mechanic, helping out in the shop."

"Well, what about Alison? When was the last time you saw her?" Marcus asked. Ryan was still trying to figure out what he wasn't telling them.

"A few days ago," Ollie said. He was still shuffling, and he shoved his hands in his jean pockets, stepping up on his toes and bouncing a bit. "She came by the garage, wanted to talk."

Ryan exchanged a glance with his brother. "About what?" he said. "Look, in case we haven't stressed this to you, Alison isn't missing just yet, but her mom is worried, and Alison's not answering. Finding her backpack up the mountain, abandoned, we have to wonder why she'd go up there, anyway. Was she looking for something, what? I'm sure you have an idea."

"Maybe she just went for a hike," Ollie said. "Did you ever think of that? She's carrying a lot of shit, you know. Maybe she just needs some space from her life, her mom, everyone. She's angry about a lot of things, angry at her mom, and then finding out the way she did that her parents had been lying to her…"

Marcus reached for his shades and pulled them down a bit on his nose, peering over them at the boy. Ollie had let something slip, and Ryan was trying to wrap his head around it. Okay, so there was a secret. He'd already figured out that much, considering how Jenny had been acting, but he had yet to find out what it was.

"About what?" Marcus said. "Come on, Ollie. Tell me everything. I guarantee you, the last thing you want is for something to happen to Alison. If she doesn't come home and I find out you withheld something that could have helped, you would be in a world of trouble. So how about this? You tell me everything you know about Alison, every-thing she told you, everything she shared, and I promise not to keep showing up here. Your other option is for me to show up at your dad's shop. I'm pretty sure he wouldn't be happy about that, considering having a cop poking around is bad for business."

He thought the kid was going to shit his pants, as he swiped both his hands over his face and dragged them down roughly. "She said she found out that her dad isn't really her dad," he said. "Something about how her parents really got into things, how her dad treated her mom, telling her what to do all the time, and then her dad was drunk one night after one of their fights. Apparently it would get pretty rough. She confronted him, told him to stop hurting her mom or something like that, and she said he just stared at her from behind his desk, and it was there in the way he looked at her.

"He told her he had a lot of regrets. He started talking and saying weird stuff, that her mom should have been more grateful to him and a bunch of weird and cryptic shit like that. She said her dad was different, changed, and she saw how scared her mom had become of him, the way he talked to her, treated her. Apparently he said something in his drunken stupor, told her that her mom had been knocked up by some guy she hooked up with before him, that she wasn't really his. But he said he'd wanted her, he'd married her mom and raised Alison as his own. Alison was gutted and upset and furious with her mom, realizing that they'd lied to her the entire time she was growing up. She felt unwanted, and she's been trying to find out who her real father is."

Ryan couldn't pull his gaze from Ollie. His heart thumped. It seemed he was getting a bigger picture of how this girl's life had crumbled apart, and maybe an idea of why she was acting like a kid from the wrong side of the tracks, doing and saying the things she was. It was because of how bad she was hurting. That was a shitty thing for a kid to hear. He crossed his arms over his chest, taking in Marcus, who glanced his way.

"So she's angry and hurt?" Marcus said. "What does that have to do with her having your old backpack and us finding it dumped up the trail with her cell phone in it?"

Ryan didn't pull his gaze from the kid, who was still shuffling and running his hands over his forehead, brushing his hair back, shaking his head. His face had peach fuzz. He knew way more about Alison and her situation than he was letting on.

"All I know is what she told me," Ollie said, still shuffling his feet. "I'm not lying to you. She's looking for him."

"Her father, her real father?" Ryan jumped in.

"That's what I said."

"Where is she looking for him? Come on, she had to have told you."

Ollie looked over to him with light hazel eyes in an unsmiling face. "Well, here, of course."

For a second, he felt his chest squeeze. "Here? You mean Livingston?"

"That's what I said. Alison told me that whoever her father is, he lives here in Livingston. That's what her dad said to her. He said her father is from Livingston, Montana. So imagine her surprise when her mom up and moved them back here. She's angry, furious at her mom. She said she's going to find him, this guy, whoever he is, and get in his face about abandoning her."

Ryan pulled in a breath, knowing how well that would go over. He wondered whether Jenny knew any of this. He was pretty sure she didn't, but then, what did he really know about the two of them other than the fact that they both seemed to be steeped heavily in secrets, likely ones they were keeping from each other?

"What does that have to do with Alison hiking up Livingston Peak?" Marcus said. "Her mom said she hates everything about the outdoors. That's what I don't understand. You said her father is here, but who is he?"

Ryan looked at his brother, realizing both of them had the same thought, that maybe she'd found him and that was where she was.

Ollie smiled, actually laughed under his breath. "She never said who the guy is. Maybe she knows, maybe she doesn't. I don't know. Her being on a hike probably has got nothing to do with that. You're right that she doesn't fit in here. The outdoorsy thing isn't for her. She talks about going back to Atlanta, too, the life she had there, the friends, the city. She misses it." He shrugged. "I have no idea what she's doing up there, but maybe she's looking to clear her head, go for a hike. Take your pick. I told Alison it was something I liked to do. Took her up there once on the back of my ATV. I like Alison, but at the same time, I know there's no rhyme or reason to anything she does."

Ryan lifted his gaze, looking past Ollie to the tilted porch.

"Okay, thanks, Ollie," Marcus said, then handed him a card. "If you hear from Alison, you call me."

Ollie took it and said nothing else as he strode up the steps, which creaked under him, and went back into the trailer.

"You think any of that's true?" Marcus asked as they started back to their vehicles. "Maybe she found the guy here, or thinks she did."

"Don't know," he said. But he'd ask Jenny, just one more thing to add to the list of secrets she seemed to be carrying. Pregnant by someone here...so who was it? Someone else she'd picked up? Maybe. Considering how she'd approached him and been gone when he woke, how many others were there? "I'll ask Jenny about this guy. I'll handle it, find out who he is, and then maybe we'll find Alison."

Marcus said nothing as he pulled open the door of the cruiser, then rested his arms on the top of the car. Then he said, "You do that, but as soon as you find out who it is, you let me know. I'll talk to him. Maybe she's already showed up at home, but if she doesn't show up tonight..."

Ryan lifted his hand. "I know. We'll start looking."

He waited until his brother had driven away, then climbed into his truck and started it, knowing he still needed to stop into his office. He'd check in and tell Peters, the other ranger working the area, let him know about Alison, a troubled teen taking off into the woods. Then he planned to ask Jenny outright who the father was, because everything about this situation with his unexpected new neighbors was beginning to snowball, and it had him wondering what other deep, dark secrets Jenny was holding on to.

He was suddenly being dragged into the life of a woman he'd slept with one time and barely knew, and suddenly, he had more questions than answers.

Chapter 11

What was it about being told to sit and wait at home that reminded her so much of Wren? Her husband had had a cruel streak she'd never expected. It was in who he was, what he did, how he crushed her with his words and then built her up again. The same words had rolled off his tongue nearly every day: "Let a man handle it, and don't worry your pretty little empty head. Stick to what you're good at, the bedroom, the kitchen, and staying fit and attractive for me."

Those were just some of the many things he'd said to her, but the smile that had charmed her the first time they'd met would appear after every cutting remark, every cruel word. And then what would he do but lean in and kiss her? She had felt as if her entire life was in the palm of his hands, and he alone controlled her.

It had been horrible to be under his mercy, feeling as if her voice, her life, her confidence were continuing to shrink away. Ryan hadn't done that, but she couldn't help feeling as if Wren still had a hold over her life.

She slapped the dough on the counter and kneaded. If she didn't do something, she thought she'd lose her mind. She'd stared at the clock and swept the floor already as she waited, listening for every creak or noise outside that would tell her Alison was home. She pictured the minute, the relief that would come, and then she'd scream and yell at her daughter for what she'd put her through yet again.

She heard a vehicle and a door closing, and she grabbed a towel, wiped her hands, and hurried barefoot to the door, ready to grab her daughter, hug her, and then yell at her. But it was only Ryan. His heavy footsteps creaked on the porch as she pushed open the screen door. He pulled off his shades and tucked them in his shirtfront, and she found herself looking around him for Alison. No one was there.

He reached for the edge of the screen door, holding it open above her head.

"You didn't find her," she said.

He just shook his head and somehow maneuvered her back into the house. "No, but we talked with Ollie, and at least we have some ideas now. Seems your daughter shared some personal stuff with him about your late husband and you, and I kind of need to ask you about it, because it could definitely tell us where Alison is. Certainly tells us where her head is at."

She didn't know what to say. Just hearing that he knew something about her, that Alison had been sharing their personal stuff with strangers, had her feeling such anger and betrayal. What was her daughter thinking?

"I can tell by your face that I've just hit a nerve, but I need you to put it aside."

She forced herself to swallow past the lump in her throat as she clutched the dish towel still in her hands. They were standing in the entryway, by the stairs. The hardwood floor was stained, and the beige carpet runner on the stairs was old and worn. Ryan was watching her as if he knew something she wasn't going to like.

"Just say it, Ryan, because I'm not liking this game of silence. It's something my husband, Wren, used to do. I'd walk on eggshells around him because he'd make me think he knew some secret about me and then wouldn't tell me. He'd let me worry about how bad it could be. It's the kind of thing that fucks with your head, so just spill it already!" she snapped. "This is my daughter. Just tell me. Whatever she said, just say it." She could feel the edge of her nerves, the bite, the discomfort.

What did he do but glance away? His expression was off, but he nodded. "It seems your daughter shared a lot about the personal problems between you and your husband. A lot of fights, anger, control. Apparently he was drunk one night and told your daughter he wasn't her father."

Had the floor actually moved? As she stared up at Ryan, it took another second before her brain reminded her she needed to breathe.

"I can tell by your face that part of that is true," he continued. "Her father also apparently told her that whoever fathered her lives here, in Livingston. Now she's looking for him. Is this true? Right now, that's the biggest lead we have, and chances are whoever this guy is, if we find him, we find Alison. Who is it, Jenny?"

She wondered whether that sound had been her, the squeaky wheeze. She had to tell herself to pull it together past the fear, the horror. Her chest tightened, and she couldn't pull her gaze from Ryan as her mind completely blanked. The man she'd married and loved…she now realized he had betrayed her.

"Are you sure he said that, that my daughter really said

that? That can't be true," she said. It was all she managed to get out, flustered, not making any sense. She'd held on to the secret for so long that she had never imagined it would come out this way. No, she'd never planned for it to come out at all. It was supposed to stay buried forever.

"So you're saying the story is made up, that Alison's father isn't someone who lives here, that your husband wouldn't have said that to her?"

"Wren was a lot of things, but hurting Alison like that is something he wouldn't have done. He loved her. I can't see him doing or saying that," she replied. No, he'd gone out of his way to put Alison first, to love her first, to love her more and do things for her that he'd never have done for Jenny. This made no sense.

"So you're saying it's a lie, that Wren is her father, her biological father?"

If she lied, would he believe her? She hesitated. The way he looked at her, really looked at her, she had to look away. "He was her father in all that mattered. He raised her, she has his name…"

"You're still not getting it. Your daughter's missing, and these secrets are going to keep us from finding her. So Wren isn't her biological father?"

It was a surreal moment, but she shook her head. "No, he's not," she finally said.

Ryan made a sound of frustration and rested both hands on his hips. He still didn't know the truth. She could see he was thinking it was someone else. It would be easy enough to let him believe that. He gave her everything. "Why is it so hard for you to just tell the truth, Jenny? Does her biological father live here, or did he? What's his name?"

She was furious at Wren for opening this door, the same door he once had closed. How could he have told

Alison when he'd been the one to say she'd never know? She swallowed again and nodded. "Yes, he's from here." She didn't pull her gaze from Ryan, seeing his frustration with her. That was a look Wren often had given her, every time they were in the same room.

"Name," Ryan said. "Come on, who is he? Chances are that's where Alison is." He pulled his cell phone out, holding it, apparently ready to make a call.

She pulled in another breath, feeling the seconds tick by, seeing the way Ryan peered at her now, hard, expecting, that alpha look that said he was waiting, and not patiently. "Well, I doubt very much Alison is with him," she said.

Confusion crossed his face before he let out a rough laugh. She was pushing every one of his buttons, something Wren had said was not one of her best qualities. "For the love of God, Jenny, just tell me who it is. Because right now, we don't know where she is, and Alison could very well be walking into a situation that could land her in more trouble."

"She's not with him!" she shouted, then shut her eyes, her hands fisted. Her chest heaved.

"And why would you say that?" he replied. It was there in the way he said it, in the edge to his voice—the realization.

"Because you're standing right here in front of me," she finally said, "and Alison isn't."

Yes, there it was in his expression, the expression of a man who'd just heard the one thing he'd never expected.

Chapter 12

Ryan couldn't help thinking this was a sick joke. Not only was Alison turning everyone's lives upside down, but now Jenny was saying he was in fact her father? Jenny was fucking with him. This couldn't possibly be true.

He stared at the woman he'd slept with…how many years ago? The exact date was murky, and he couldn't get his head around how truly messed up this was. He waited for a smile, for something, but all she did was appear uncomfortable.

"What?" was all he managed to get out. At the same time, his cell phone started to ring, and Marcus's name was on the screen. He should answer it, but he wasn't sure he could speak.

"Who is it?" Jenny asked.

He accepted the call and put the phone to his ear. He couldn't talk to her right now. When he answered, his voice sounded so off even to him. "Yeah?"

"Did you find out from Jenny about the father?" Marcus said.

He shut his eyes and pressed his thumb and finger to the bridge of his nose to pull it together. He couldn't shake the sick feeling in his stomach. "Yeah, listen, let me call you right back," he said and hung up the phone before his brother could say anything else. Then he turned back to Jenny and jabbed his index finger at her. "Go back to the beginning and tell me everything, and no fucking around, Jenny. Did you just say I'm Alison's father? That the one night we had sex, you got pregnant, and she's mine? Did you just seriously say that?"

He knew he sounded accusatory, like an asshole. Something in her expression seemed, hurt, scared, or maybe she was guilty at having been caught in a lie.

"Let's be clear on something, Ryan," she said. "You may be the biological father, but that's all you were. Wren was her father. I can't believe he told her. It was him who never wanted her to know. I found out I was pregnant after I was with him. It wasn't a big deal. It was…"

"Not a big deal! Are you kidding me? How could you not have told me? I had a right to know." He leaned in, got in her face, and the way he yelled, he felt fury oozing from him, shooting up from the ground and all the way through him. He couldn't remember ever feeling this angry before.

"You're upset," she said.

Was she for real? "Oh, I'm a little more than that. Why would you do it?"

She said nothing. He could tell she was struggling to come up with something that would explain this.

"Does Alison know I'm her father?" he asked. He wasn't sure why she was looking at him the way she was, with confusion. Loss seemed to fill her brown eyes, turning them to big dark pools that showed every emotion. What kind of screwed-up life had she had? Then she shook her head.

"I didn't even know she knew. I can't believe Wren did that, not to Alison. He'd hurt me, but why her? I…" She lifted her hand, still clutching a dish towel, and he found himself looking around at the house that had belonged to Althea. It had the same furnishings he remembered, the aged burgundy sofa that looked practically new, the matching chair, the tables, the blankets, the art on the wall of nature and landscapes, the photos of generations of family he'd never taken the time to really look at.

"Well, evidently, he told her," he said. "So Wren knew about me. Let's assume he told her my name, yet I've heard nothing from her."

Jenny pulled her lower lip between her teeth as if thinking. She looked down and away before shaking her head, then lifting her gaze and giving him everything. "I never told Wren your name. He said he didn't want to know." Her voice was soft, and for maybe the first time, he believed she was telling him the truth. "I gave him an out, but he said he didn't want it, that it didn't matter I was pregnant. He'd take us both."

"But he knew something about me, or didn't he?"

She went to say something, then shook her head. "Would he have found out? Maybe, likely. He was always finding out everything about people. Said that was what gave him the upper hand, to know the secrets of his enemies and everyone around him. He kept files," she said, crossing her arms under her breasts and pulling in a breath that had her chest heaving.

He just stared at her, sensing that her husband may have had a dark and dangerous side. He could be wrong, but it was just a feeling he couldn't shake from the little she'd said.

"After he…" She gestured vaguely, and he heard her hesitation before she continued. "After he died, I went through his office, a room in our house that I'd never gone in. I hadn't been allowed. He was always there. His desk was glass, with a drawer he always kept locked. I busted the lock with a crowbar I found in the garage. I was looking for insurance papers, a will, something after the first notice showed up for foreclosure on the house. Wren had handled everything, and here I was now, trying to figure out how to manage on my own with my daughter. I had no money because Wren was the sole breadwinner, and I'm not kidding when I say he looked after everything, no discussions, nothing.

"I was completely in the dark about what he did, what he had. The bank accounts were in his name, the credit cards, the house. As I was looking for everything, I found files on the people he worked with. He had dug up dirt on each of them, things from their pasts, things they'd done, secrets about their characters and their finances. He had done the same thing with all of them, so would he have done it with me?" She was pacing now, and all he could think was to wonder what kind of life she'd given his daughter. "If I'm being honest with myself, he likely would have, because Wren didn't trust anyone. I discovered there was a lot more to my husband, a side of him I didn't know anything about. But why didn't Alison say anything to me? It makes no sense."

As he squeezed his phone and took in the house, he wondered how much Jenny really wanted to know. Sometimes women found it easier to look the other way, as if avoiding the truth was the answer to everything.

"Then let's assume she knows about me—or maybe she doesn't. Where're your husband's files, his papers? Do you still have them here?"

She was already shaking her head. "No. The house was taken by the bank, and the IRS demanded back taxes.

He'd leveraged everything. I put most of it in storage, his papers, his things. I mean, there was no need for me to keep it, and what would that have to do with finding Alison?" She lifted her hands and then let them fall to her sides. "I walked away from that life when my aunt left me this house. I didn't even know her, but it was a gift, a new start, a way to break away. I didn't want anything of him."

It seemed she was trying to explain away what she had done. At the same time, if Wren had dirt on him, he wanted to know what it was and what he could possibly have shared with Alison. It would be hard to undo the damage if someone had trashed his character.

"I think I'll start with her room," Ryan said. "Have you searched her room? She likely has something there that will give us an idea of where she is, where her head is, and what she knows. Right now, if she's looking for me, what she's doing makes no sense, so I don't think she knows. Actually, I'm sure she doesn't, because I'm right next door, and nothing she's said or done so far since I've met her tells me she thought I was her father. So take me up to my daughter's room." He wasn't asking, and the way her mouth opened and closed, he could see she was rattled.

"Just one thing, Ryan. I'm her mother. She's my daughter, and Wren is her father."

He shook his head and leaned in. "You're wrong there, Jenny. She's my daughter too, a daughter you never gave me the opportunity to know, so let's get that straight—and Wren doesn't sound like the kind of guy who was much of a father. He tried to hurt her by telling her she wasn't his. That's not what a father does. So, first things first. Show me her room, and when I find her, things are going to change."

Her expression hardened, flickering with anger.

"Sounds to me like you're trying to tell me what to do," she said.

"No, that's not what I'm doing. Now that I know she's my daughter, the truth is coming out. I'll find her, and then I'll figure out what I can do to help her, to have a relationship with her, to straighten this mess out. And you and I…" He let the words hang, knowing it was the anger speaking. "Not sure where we go, but I know you've spoken your last lie to me."

Her face paled, and she nodded before starting to the stairs, though she stopped halfway up and looking back at him. "I never expected this to happen, Ryan. I'm sorry," she said. She pulled in another breath. "Her room's up here, first door at the top of the stairs."

Then she kept going, and Ryan took another second to pull it together before starting up, one foot in front of the other, wondering how he was going to explain this to his brother.

Chapter 13

Okay, so the secret was out. The one thing she'd feared was now the elephant in the room, and she couldn't shake the feeling of being despised, hated. Could she blame Ryan?

She took a second in her bathroom to pull it together. Marcus had shown up at the door, and she'd overheard Ryan telling him that he was Alison's father. In the second of silence that followed, Marcus had given him a look that said everything about the bomb he had dropped.

She was still shaken by the way Marcus had looked over at her.

What had she done then but slip away into the bathroom? She splashed water on her face and stared in the mirror at the image staring back, wondering when everything in her life had turned to shit. She couldn't remember the exact moment it had happened, when the person she had been slowly slipped away and became the person Wren had created. He had toyed with everything about who she really was and what had made her tick, manipulating and destroying her. How could a man say he loved her when everything he did told her he hated her?

And here, now, her daughter was the casualty.

She pulled open the bathroom door, fisting her hands as she stepped out into the hallway, seeing the open stairs and hearing Ryan and Marcus's voices coming from her daughter's room at the end of the hall. She pictured her daughter's face, seeing for the first time why she was so angry. *Damn you, Wren. How could you be so cruel?*

"Holy fuck, Ryan," Marcus was saying. "Are you one hundred percent sure she's yours? This is so totally fucked up. This is just…"

She stopped just outside the door, her heart zigging and her stomach zagging and she listened to one more man questioning her character. She shouldn't listen, but her feet wouldn't move.

"Would make sense," Ryan muttered, still pissed off.

"I still can't believe the fate at play here. This entire time, a woman you slept with years ago was related to Althea Kunkel. Now you find out you knocked her up, and she had a kid and a fucked-up marriage to a man who told his daughter she wasn't his. Like, what kind of asshole does that? Then they move in next door to you. Holy shit, Ryan. You really have a way of picking the most screwed-up women and finding yourself in situations no normal person would find himself in. Let me know when you tell Mom and everyone, because I want a front-row seat to the show when you try to explain this."

She thought he was making a joke at her expense, and she forced herself to take another step. The floor creaked as she stood in the doorway, and both men turned to face her. Marcus was going through Alison's bedside table, pulling out books and journals and papers she hadn't even known her daughter had. Ryan was holding a blue journal, reading it.

"I can assure you, Marcus, Alison is his," Jenny said. "Yes, you're right: My marriage was fucked up, my life is fucked up, I'm fucked up, but I had no idea Wren would try to hurt Alison the way he did. Up until then, I had been the one he used as a punching bag for his words. I can also assure you I couldn't have been more surprised to find out that Ryan lives right next door. This is a mess, so if you two are done trashing my character, tell me if you've found anything. Did she know about you, Ryan? Does it say anything in there?"

She didn't miss the exchange between the brothers, but she wasn't going to sneak off again and hide. She'd done that for too many years. She'd had a fresh start now. This was supposed to have been a new life for just her and her daughter, only Alison was doing everything she could not to come on board. At least now Jenny had some idea why.

"No, nothing, but it seems she has a lot of anger issues," Ryan said. "There's a lot here to read through, but at the same time, if she doesn't come home soon…"

Marcus had basically emptied the entire drawer, and he pulled out a red diary shoved way in the back, the kind that had a lock on it. "There's this," he said and held it up. "Do you mind?"

Ryan pulled what looked like a jackknife from his belt and flicked it open. "Yeah," was all he said before cutting the lock away from the book, and she felt the slap. It felt as if another man was making another decision for her.

"Yes, by all means, to find my daughter," she said as she stepped into the room. "A little respect, Ryan. I've been down this road once before with Wren, and I won't be handled as if I have no voice. Ask me. Don't dismiss me."

She wasn't sure what look passed between Ryan and Marcus, maybe because all she could feel was anger.

"My mistake," Ryan said. "That wasn't my intention, Jenny. Don't jump to conclusions. Right now, we're just trying to find Alison. Once she's back here, then we can sort some things out between you and me, between you and Alison. We'll sit down, the three of us, and lay all the cards on the table. By no means am I trying to treat you as if you have no voice, so don't accuse me of that. At the same time, I don't know what you went through or what Alison went through, because you won't talk about it. Your husband died. You said he was shot—how, why, where? With all of this going on, I have to wonder, what really happened? What went down? But as I said, that discussion is for after we find her, after she comes home. We can sit her down and—"

"Ryan," Marcus said. He was reading the red journal and flipped to a page before pushing the small book over to him. Her heart was hammering.

"What the fuck…?" Ryan muttered under his breath, reading whatever it was, another secret she didn't know about.

"What is it? Seriously," she said, walking closer.

Ryan's expression changed to alarm as he flicked his gaze over to her. "She knows her father is an O'Connell, but she thinks it's Luke, my brother. How, I don't know. Shit, dammit…"

Jenny dragged her gaze from one brother to the other. "Fill me in. Who's Luke, exactly?"

"Our brother, home from the military," Marcus said.

Ryan walked the book over to her and held it up, turning it so she could see her daughter's scrawl. She'd never known she was journaling. She took in the words that were double underlined.

I found him, Luke, my father. Ollie was right that it's time to face the music. Can't wait to meet him, to talk to him. Let's see if he's exactly the asshole my dad said he'd be.

She read it again, staring in horror.

"I have to ask, Jenny...did you hook up with my brother, too?" Ryan said.

For a second, she was too stunned to answer. "You're serious?" Her voice squeaked, and even Marcus seemed embarrassed. She pushed back her shoulders, lifted her chin, and looked at one brother, then the other. There was no damn way she would let either of them make her feel less than. She was done with that. "I have no idea who your brother is. I do know exactly who fathered her, and that's you. It would be easier for me to say it wasn't. In fact, I'd prefer it," she snapped, but as she took in Ryan, she saw it in that second, there in his face. She didn't think he believed her.

Chapter 14

Jenny had insisted on coming with him and was now in the passenger side of his pickup, having changed into a pair of blue jeans and sneakers, her hair pulled back in a ponytail. The sun had now dipped lower on the horizon. She'd said no more than two words to Ryan since he'd accused her of having slept with Luke.

He couldn't explain it, but reading the words, thoughts, and feelings Alison had recorded privately in her diary had felt like such a betrayal of her. From the little he'd read, he'd been able to feel her confusion and anger.

The tension in the truck was absolutely thick as he pulled up in front of his mom's house, where he expected Luke to be. Marcus was already there, likely inside, his cruiser parked in the driveway behind the pickup.

Ryan took in Jenny in the passenger seat. She was silent and had pulled into herself. It was the same behavior he recognized from his mom and his sisters when they were hurting and didn't want to talk. Before he'd turned off the truck, she had already opened her door to step out.

"Jenny," he said, "this is about Alison first, about finding her. Then I want to know everything, everything that happened with Wren. I want you to open up and talk, but I can see the lack of trust you have. Maybe you think everyone is going to hurt you like he did, but that's not true."

She stilled her hand on the open door.

"I guess I just don't understand why you stayed," he said. "You said he hurt you, and you let him. I guess I don't understand why you wouldn't just walk away and leave him, at least for Alison."

She pulled in a breath, her chest rising. He could see how tightly she held herself as she turned to him, her face filled with raw emotion, her deep brown eyes so angry. "I can't make you understand," she said. "It was just something that happened. Falling for someone, everything was perfect—and then it wasn't. A numb feeling came over me when I suddenly realized that nothing would ever be right again. I was educated and smart, and I didn't even realize I was so desperate and lonely that I'd let a man do that to me, treat me like that, have that kind of power over me.

"I don't know how it happened. I was just suddenly in it, living it. It was my life, and one day it changed. Everything about him was different. There was the drinking, and he was so powerful. He said I owed him. He said, 'I don't mean to yell, but why do you make me do what I do to you? You make everything so damn hard. Just get down on your knees, where you belong.'

"He was so loving in the beginning, and then something just snapped and changed along the way. It became about Alison, staying because of her, not having the strength to walk out because I didn't believe it was something I could do. Instead, I listened to every cruel remark, believing what he said. Near the end, I heard him laugh when he showed more of who he was. He said I was vulnerable, lonely, fucking weak. It was my fault. I had made it too easy.

"It was the mind games, the way he believed he owned me, every part of me. After he was shot, when I stared at the blood on my hands, you know what? It was a relief. I was so happy he was dead, because for the first time, I could breathe. At the same time, I loved him, and I was angry at that part of me that could still love him despite who he was.

"I have a mother and father, you know, brothers and sisters. I don't see them anymore because he didn't want it, didn't want me in their lives or them in mine. I haven't spoken to them in so many years. He isolated me, and I let him. You think I'm a liar? You demand the truth? Well, I won't be treated like that or have you look down on me because you believe I'm the worst mother ever, because I stayed in the marriage, because I wasn't strong enough, because I didn't do the best in your eyes. You're right. I don't trust anyone, and it shouldn't matter to me what you think. Is there anything else you want to know?" Passion flickered in the way she spoke.

In that moment, as she shared her dark night of the soul, he realized it was a part of her. It was there in her voice, something so raw. Knowing just how vulnerable she was had him understanding more of what her life had been, and his daughter's. What they'd lived through, he didn't understand.

"You said your husband was shot, but you haven't said what happened," he finally said. "Who shot him, how, why?" He unfastened his seatbelt. Marcus was standing in the doorway, gesturing to him. Jenny looked straight ahead, out the window, and he didn't have to see her eyes to know how hurt she had to be.

She said nothing for another second, then gave him everything in the next breath. "I was upstairs in our bedroom when I heard the gunshot. It took me a minute to understand what it was that I had heard. I raced down the stairs and into his office, seeing him on the floor, bleeding, and my daughter was standing there. I remember going to him, seeing the look in his eyes—horror, fear, something I'd never seen before. I pressed my hands to his stomach as I tried to stop the bleeding. I screamed at her to call 911, but she just stood there, and it was then, as I looked at her, hearing Wren gasping and feeling his body jerk under me, that I realized she was staring at him. There was a gun in her hand, at her side. I could feel the life pouring out of him."

His chest tightened. She looked away for a second, and he wondered if the horror he was feeling showed. Things were going from bad to worse for his kid.

"But she didn't answer me," Jenny continued. "She just backed away, dropped the gun to the floor, and walked out of the room. I called 911 and watched the life seep out of him. When I heard the sirens coming, I knew he was dead, and all I could think of was protecting my kid, so I picked up the gun, knowing I was out of time. I didn't think. I just ran into the kitchen, and the first thing I thought of was the grease trap under the sink. I grabbed the dishtowel and lifted the lid, and I slid the gun in, pushing it into the white, solidified grease. It just fit, and it was hidden. Then I put the lid back. I don't remember ever feeling so clear or confident as I focused everything in each moment. I heard pounding at the door, and I hurried back to where Wren was lying in a pool of blood. I just yelled and called out as I went back down on my knees with the towel still in my hand, and I pressed it to the hole in his chest, covering it with blood even though it was no longer spilling out. That was where they found me.

"Of course, they knew he was dead. They pulled me off him. They tried to revive him, loading him in the ambulance. The police were there. I said it had to have been a break-in or someone he was meeting with. I said I'd heard the shot and had found him, and I had no idea what had happened. I grabbed Alison from her room, and we went to the hospital. All the while, the cops were at the house, and I knew they were searching, investigating. The entire time, I was picturing where I hid the gun, right there in plain sight in the grease trap. They never found it. They said there were no signs of a break-in, so it had to have been someone he knew. Wren had a lot of visitors, men, people he did business with. The neighbors were questioned and said there was always a lot of coming and going. He worked from home."

Then she stopped talking and stepped out of the truck, and she stood there and faced him. He didn't have a clue what to say.

"So now you know my secret, and you know something no one else does, Ryan," she said. "You wanted to know something? Well, that something gives you the ammunition to blow my world apart, and my daughter's. There, now you know everything, or more than anyone knows. Now, if you don't mind, I want to find her."

She shut the door, and all Ryan could do as he stepped out of the truck, following a woman he knew nothing about, was try to wrap his head around the fact that his daughter had shot the man who raised her.

Now he was left with more questions than answers. What the hell had happened in that room between Wren and Alison, and why?

Chapter 15

Iris O'Connell was a tiny woman, maybe five feet, with the same blue eyes as her son. Actually, every one of the O'Connells seemed to have the same vibrant blue eyes.

She was in Ryan's mother's home, sitting in a chair in the living room after meeting Luke, who had long dark hair, a ripped body, and eyes that gave everything when he looked at her. Iris was sitting on the sofa beside Jenny in capris and a white tank. Her dark hair was short, and her face gave away nothing of what she was thinking. She was polite. Jenny felt out of place.

"As I said, Alison is my daughter," Ryan said, "and she's missing. Jenny and I were together once. I didn't know about Alison. They just moved here from Atlanta. Marcus and I found in her journal that she knows her father is an O'Connell, but she believes it's Luke. There's nothing else you need to know right now."

There was something odd about having everything summed up in a paragraph. No one said anything, as the front door opened just then, and a woman called out, "Hey! Didn't know everyone was showing up here today. What's the occasion? Why didn't anyone…?" She was short, with red hair and the same brilliant blue eyes, wearing a black pantsuit. As she stepped into the living room, she stopped talking, likely at the sight of the shock that Jenny knew was on all their faces.

Luke didn't pull his gaze from Ryan. "I'm not understanding," he said. "You're saying you have a kid with your neighbor, the girl who was causing trouble next door, and now she's missing because she's gone searching for her father, who is actually you, but she thinks it's me?" He gestured between her and Ryan.

The redheaded woman glanced at her in shock, then at Ryan. "You have a kid?" she said. She had to be a sister. Her voice was dramatic, high pitched. How many sisters had Ryan said there were?

"Okay, manners, here," Iris said. "Karen, this is Jenny. Yes, apparently I have a grandchild, and we're just trying to sort out the situation. It's kind of a mess. Everyone is understandably upset, but we need to focus. This is about finding Alison."

Karen closed her mouth and dragged her gaze over to Jenny, who didn't have any idea what she was thinking. Sitting here with this family, she could feel herself shrinking under the spotlight shining down on her. Uncomfortable was an understatement.

"Okay, I guess it's nice to meet you, Jenny," Karen said, then gave her attention back to her brothers, who towered over her. "I have a ton of questions here, like…you didn't know? How old is she? And what the hell happened?"

"Karen, I'm sure everyone has a ton of questions," Ryan said, "but right now, all that matters is finding Alison.

Whatever questions you have will have to wait. But yes, she's my kid, actually a teenager. Luke, you're saying no kid has come around here or tried to reach out to you? She's about this high, short dark hair that looks like she cut it herself…" Ryan held his hand up to show her height.

"She did cut it herself," Jenny said, "and dyed her hair just before that. It's a mess—and don't forget her nose ring."

Karen dragged her gaze over to her, and so did Luke.

Jenny shrugged. "She's going through some stuff." She couldn't make herself look at Ryan as she said it, because she didn't want to see the way he was looking at her, what he thought of her, what a horrible person she was.

"Karen is a lawyer, Jenny," he said in a way that surprised her, and she wasn't sure what expressions she was seeing on everyone else's faces. Of course, they had to be wondering why he'd said that, or maybe it was just her own paranoia.

Then Luke was shaking his head. "I'm telling you, I haven't heard from or talked to anyone."

"Well, hang on a second, Luke," Iris said. Everyone looked her way, and she crossed her legs and rested her hand over her knee. "Didn't you say some underage teen girl was outside the liquor store, trying to get you to buy her beer?"

"When was this?" Marcus asked.

Jenny had to fight the urge to squirm, as Karen kept dragging her gaze between Ryan and her. She was still reeling over what she'd shared. Vulnerability was a constant companion she didn't want to have anymore.

"Today," he said. "Maybe sometime this afternoon." Luke had crossed his arms over his wide chest. He was wearing a gray T-shirt over blue jeans, and his muscles showed through every stitch of clothing. "Yeah, a troubled kid, a teenager, walked right up to me as I came out."

"What did she look like?" Ryan started, then turned to Jenny. "You have a photo of Alison on your phone?"

She pulled her phone from her back pocket. "I'm not sure how recent it is, not after the godawful cut…" She opened her phone, seeing the pictures of her unsmiling daughter. "Here's one from just after we moved here."

In the photo, Alison's hair was still long, but she had already dyed it jet black. Jenny didn't know why, but she showed Iris first.

"That was before she cut it all off and pierced her nose," she said. She wasn't sure what to make of Iris's expression as she held out the phone to Ryan, who showed it to Karen, Marcus, and Luke. Just watching the four siblings, she could see they were close.

"Well, that's her," Ryan said. "Boy, she really looks different there." He lifted his gaze to her. Alison had changed so much. It had been like a downward spiral, and Jenny had been at a loss for what to do.

"I don't know," Luke said. "Maybe, not sure. Yeah, short dark hair that looked like she'd butchered it—and she was dressed ridiculously slutty, looking for trouble. It was more the guy with her, though. He was tall, scrawny, and his shirt and pants…like a grease monkey. Why does she think I'm her father? No offence, but I've never seen you before," he said, turning to Jenny.

She didn't move or say anything, sitting as straight as she could as she tried to figure out how to explain the inner mind of Wren.

"We don't know all the details for sure," Ryan said. "Jenny is at a loss, as well. But this guy she was with, that sounds an awful lot like Ollie Edwards, and I'm pretty sure he told us he hadn't seen her."

Ryan and Marcus looked at each other, and then Marcus walked out of the room, his phone to his ear. She didn't know what that was about.

"We should take a ride back over to Ollie Edwards's place," Ryan said. "Luke, you should come with us." He let his gaze land back on her and gestured to her, and she stood and walked over to him. He settled his hand on her shoulder, steering her away. "Look, I'm going to head back over to Ollie's with Luke and Marcus. Can you stay here with my mom and sister? I'm not telling you what to do, and we need to talk about what happened, but in the meantime, please just stay here."

Even though she wanted to say no, she realized from the way he touched her that he was asking, not demanding. He rested his hand on her shoulder, then pulled away. She could hear his family talking behind them, but she didn't know what they were saying.

"Okay, but you call me the minute you know anything, the second you talk to him…"

He pressed his hand over her shoulder again and rubbed, then nodded. Just then, Marcus walked back in the room, and Ryan and Luke followed him out, leaving her alone with two women she didn't know. They'd have a lot of questions they'd want answered.

She pulled in a breath to say something, but Iris started toward her first.

"Okay, so who's had dinner, nobody?" she said. "Well, I have a casserole in the oven, and Luke's beer is in the fridge. Karen, pour yourself a glass of wine. Come on, you two…" She was already moving into the kitchen, and Jenny realized she hadn't even waited for them to answer.

"Wine or beer?" Karen asked her.

For a second, she stared, waiting for the inquisition. "Uh…" she said.

Karen somehow maneuvered her into the kitchen, sitting her on a stool at the island. A beer was poured in a glass in front of her, and Iris and Karen were suddenly talking about the weather, how long to cook the shepherd's pie, and whether they should add onions to the salad.

Chapter 16

"Holy shit, Ryan," Luke said. "You know how to screw the pooch big time, so to speak. You really knocked that chick up? Man, I've heard of a lot of things, but you having a kid who's, by the sounds of it, one step from juvie…"

Luke was sitting in the passenger side of his truck as he followed Marcus back to Ollie's place, his hand on the grab bar on the roof. The truck rattled over ruts in the road, and the sun had settled on the horizon. Now it was getting dark.

"Her name's Jennifer, Jenny," he replied, "and there's more to the story that I'm still trying to wrap my head around. How about we leave that for now and just find my kid? You think it was her outside the beer shop? And the timing, seriously, she just walked up to you?"

He didn't have to look over to his brother to hear him run his hands over his face, scraping over his stubble. At least he'd gotten his brother out of the house and was prompting some type of conversation.

"Yeah, maybe," Luke said. "The kid was a mess, with

the hacked-off dyed hair. I've seen some pretty bad ones, but she was wearing enough makeup and dark shadow that it seemed like she was taking up streetwalking. And what she was wearing…her shorts barely covered her, and the cut of her shirt, she may as well not have been wearing one. If that's your kid, you've got a serious problem you need to straighten out, and quick, because I'm telling you she wasn't really a kid, if you get my drift. The guy she was with, it looked like he was familiar with her in ways he shouldn't be. How old is she, anyway, seventeen, eighteen?"

He spotted the single wide and could see Marcus pulling up ahead of them. "No, almost fifteen."

"Whoa, seriously? She didn't look anywhere near that young. Maybe it wasn't her. Let's hope it wasn't."

He pulled up and parked behind his brother's cruiser. Marcus was already pounding on the door as he turned off the truck and then looked over to his brother. "Oh, it was her, unfortunately. That's what scares me."

"Man, then you're definitely going to have your hands full, with a kid who turned out like that. Walking trouble. You said there's more, but what more can there be? Did she have a father, or was it just Jenny and her?"

He knew his brother had questions. All his family would, and he knew they'd keep asking until he answered, but the problem was that he couldn't talk to them about any of it, considering what Jenny had said. Murder, messing with a crime scene, hiding the weapon and then lying…and who knew what else?

"I know you have questions, but how about we just find her? That's step one. Then, once I get my answers…"

Luke just gestured toward the trailer as he stepped out of the truck, and Ryan followed. Marcus was talking with an older man with sandy hair in a stained T-shirt and khakis. He stopped at the bottom of the stairs, hearing a

TV inside and seeing the way the man glanced from Luke over to him.

"Well, what is this about?" the man said. "Why do you want to talk to Ollie?"

He didn't miss the paranoia and suspicion in his voice. Had to be the father.

"We're looking for a friend of his, a girl by the name of Alison Sweetgrass," Marcus said, holding the door open. "We spoke with Ollie this afternoon, and we have some more questions for him. You're his father?"

Ryan rested his hand on the rail of the stairs, his foot on one of the rickety steps. He didn't have to look over to Luke to know that the way he was standing, arms crossed, was likely the reason the man appeared as unsettled as he did. It was just the effect his brother had, that perpetually pissed-off military presence. Add in a cop at the door and then him, and the man must have thought his son was in a world of shit.

"Yes, I'm Ollie's dad, Pete Edwards, but Ollie's not here. I don't know any Alison, but I don't know many of his friends. A girl, huh? So what has she done, or has she dragged my kid into something? What is this?" Yup, he sounded defensive.

"No, look, Ollie's not in trouble," Marcus said. "We've been looking for Alison. She's a missing person, is all. When we spoke with him this afternoon, he said he hadn't seen her, but we have a witness who saw them together today. Alison is a minor, too…"

Pete was already shaking his head, and Ryan knew why his brother had let the statement hang like that. "Look, I don't know where he is, but if he said he didn't see her, then your witness is wrong. You said my kid's not in trouble. He's a good kid and has a good head on his shoulders.

If he's with some girl who has a cop and ranger showing up at my door, then she's the problem…"

"She's my daughter," Ryan said. They were getting nowhere, and he could sense Pete was getting ready to point another finger at Alison or tell them to leave. "She's missing, and we're just trying to locate her. Ollie isn't in trouble, per se, unless he's hiding her. Lying to an officer, that is a problem. Do you know where your son is?"

Pete shook his head.

"Look, we just want to find her," Ryan continued, "so the best thing would be to go and get Ollie on the phone so we can settle this once and for all."

"I don't know where he is," Pete said. "I told you that. He could be in town or something. I just got home from the shop."

Ryan could see how stained his hands were, a mechanic's rough hands. The yard was overgrown, and he could just make out metal and engine parts in a wheelbarrow off to the side. An old rusted-out car had weeds growing through it, too.

"You've said that already, so how about you get Ollie on the phone now?" Marcus said, though it wasn't a question.

It was another second before Pete walked back inside, and Marcus stood in the doorway, holding the screen door open. He heard the TV turn off, and then he could hear the man talking on the phone.

"Hey, Ollie, it's Dad. Where are you? Because there's a couple cops here, and a ranger. They said they spoke with you earlier about a girl…" He appeared in the doorway again, the phone to his ear.

Pete wasn't soft spoken, and Ryan could just make out someone on the other end. It had to be Ollie. He could feel his heart hammering. He was getting answers, and he hoped to God Alison was with the boy. He glanced over to Luke, who was standing with his arms crossed, still holding his ground.

"What's the girl's name again?" Pete asked Marcus, pulling the phone away from his ear.

"Alison," Marcus said. "Is that Ollie on the phone? Let me talk to him."

"Hey, Ollie, this cop wants to talk to you. Listen, you tell him where she is. Then you come on home, you hear?" Pete said, then handed Marcus the phone.

"Ollie, this is Deputy O'Connell. I spoke with you only a few hours ago, and you said you hadn't seen Alison, but we have a witness putting you outside the liquor store. You two were trying to hustle beer."

Ryan couldn't hear what the kid was saying to his brother.

"Cut the crap, Ollie," Marcus replied. "Where is she? You want to help her, then you tell us where she is."

Marcus was listening again and shook his head as he lifted his gaze to Ryan, who wanted to take the phone and find out where Ollie was and what was going on with Alison. Given what Jenny said had happened, he was no longer just worried about his kid being out there. Now, a life sentence was hanging in the shadows. She could end up locked away forever, and he didn't have a clue when the details of that night could be coming to bite her in the ass.

"Then you stay there," Marcus said. "We're coming now." He hung up the phone and handed it back to Pete. "I'm going out there now. Your son's not in trouble. Thanks for co-operating. Alison is with Ollie."

Ryan stepped back with his brother, falling in beside Marcus as they moved back to their vehicles.

"Apparently, it was Alison and Ollie outside the store," Marcus said. "He took her up into the park on his ATV, to some shelter he found or something. He'll meet us at the trailhead."

Ryan glanced back to the now closed door of the trailer, feeling as if he was finally getting closer to fixing this. "Before we go, can you find out everything about a shooting in Atlanta? It was Jenny's husband, Wren Sweetgrass," he said. "This may go nowhere, but I have a feeling that after we find Alison, there could be another bigger problem lurking on the horizon."

He had his brothers' attention.

"Uh, yeah, I can, but I'm almost afraid to ask why," Marcus said, and Luke said nothing, just wiped his face. Ryan knew that anything he said would stay just between them.

"Jenny just told me something else that I don't know how to wrap my head around," he said. "It appears her husband's shooting wasn't an accident. Alison may have shot him, and Jenny may have covered it up. I have no idea where this sits with the Atlanta PD."

Chapter 17

J enny had taken only a few sips of the beer when another woman walked in the back door of the kitchen, wearing a dark blue firefighter's uniform. Her long dark hair was tied back, and she was several inches taller than both Karen and Iris. Her name was Suzanne, the other sister, and from the ensuing conversation, Jenny realized there was also another brother, Owen, who was the eldest, a plumber. For some reason, she stared at the back door, expecting him to walk in too as she waited for word from Ryan.

"That's the third time you've glanced at your phone," Iris said. "Ryan will call as soon as they hear something. Drink your beer." The woman was confident and gorgeous, and Jenny could see the resemblance that linked all the O'Connells—the same expressions, the same eyes. "So would you tell me about Alison?"

Suzanne and Karen stood across from her, leaning against the counter by the sink. The wall oven was on, and she could smell the casserole. The aroma should have had her mouth watering, but her appetite had fled. Her daughter having gone inconsiderately missing had left her anxious and out of sorts.

"Yes, Alison. Well, she's a teenager, fourteen, born April 8. She's headstrong and smart, but as of late, I never know what to expect from her."

All three were giving her everything, and she waited for the questions about her character, about how she could have kept Alison from Ryan. She expected it, but instead there was only interest.

"Ah, those teenage years," Iris said. "I know them well. I did it alone with six kids. They can test everything you have and then some, your sanity, your peace of mind. Then there're the sleepless nights. They're at that age where they're no longer sweet little kids, and they suddenly believe they know everything, more than you. I understand well that battle for independence and sense of self." Iris actually reached over and patted her hand, then gestured to the beer that was still full in front of her. "You know, Luke was the one who took off on me. He camped out in those hills, not just once, but every time he was fine— better than fine, as a matter of fact. That was maddening, considering I was a wreck. I swore it took ten years off me."

"It was five times, Mom," Karen said, then lifted her glass of white wine and took a sip. "He actually built a shelter for himself. He went up to sleep in it and kept food there, said it was the place he went when he needed to think. Guess that should've been a sign he would join the military, special forces. He learned early how to go it alone, and he always came back. Wonder if that's why he stays here now when he's on leave, because of how he made everything so hard for you, Mom."

Suzanne had her arms crossed, and the way she was looking at Jenny, long and hard, made her wonder if the criticism was coming, but Suzanne merely pulled her gaze from her and slid it over to Karen and her mom. "And then there was you, Karen," she said. "The way you butted heads with Mom…good God, thought you'd bring the house down around all of us. I was the good one. Then there was Owen, who acted like the parent, the responsible one."

Jenny found herself looking around at Karen, Suzanne, and Iris, who cringed.

"Let's just say I survived, and I have every right to the early gray in my hair, which I now have to color regularly," Iris said. "Honestly, I think all of you should forever be picking up the bill for it."

"Aw, Mom, you don't look a day over thirty…thirty-five…forty," Karen said, teasing.

Iris tossed her a frown, and Jenny wondered if this was a joke between them. "We totally get the teenage girl thing," she said. "Don't worry, though. Ryan knows the woods, the park, and with Luke and Marcus, they'll find her. She'll be home in no time to continue driving you crazy and testing you, doing more stupid teenage stuff, and you'll find yourself counting the days until the next crisis."

Okay, not what she'd expected. She reached for her beer, lifted it, and took a swallow. "You're being rather nice," she said, "considering Ryan is Alison's father. I kind of expected anger at me for keeping it from him, not telling him. At the same time, it was just one of those things. We'd barely exchanged names. I had already met my husband and started seeing him by the time I found out I was pregnant." She made herself stop talking, watching the exchange between the women.

"So your husband is in the picture, or not?" Karen asked, leaning on the island. "You live next door to Ryan, just you and your daughter?"

All three seemed to lean in closer, waiting for what she'd say. The question was there on their faces. She could always see when someone was curious. It was right there.

"No, he's not in the picture," she said. "He died. It's just me and my daughter."

There it was, the sympathy.

She felt herself wanting to share more, but that wasn't a good idea, so she pulled her gaze away and stared at her beer. "And here we are. Imagine my surprise at moving in right next to Ryan, but now my daughter's missing. As you know, she's been rather prickly…"

"Understandably so," Iris said. "Oh, I'm so sorry for your loss."

Suzanne was studying her in a way that was making her uncomfortable. She fought the urge to roll her shoulders.

"I guess I'm at a loss as to why she thinks Luke is her father, though," Karen said, swirling her wine in her glass.

Jenny could feel the minute the questions had started to spin in a direction she didn't like. All three women were giving her everything. Now would've been a perfect time for Ryan to call, to come back and walk through the door, or for the roof to fall in.

"You know what?" Iris said. "It's not the time for twenty questions or for poking and prodding into Jenny's personal life. This is really between Ryan and Jenny," she added to Suzanne and Karen—though, as Suzanne's eyes were once again glued on Jenny, she wasn't sure she agreed.

"You know, Jenny," Iris continued, "one of the things I learned the hard way is that when you're a single parent, everyone suddenly believes they can tell you how to raise your kids. They point out how you can do better, or they become quick to criticize when your kid screws up. I had six, so you can multiply the comments you've heard about your kid to have some idea of what I was on the receiving end of. Not sure it's gotten any better now, but don't let anyone make you feel as if you're the one screwing up. There's a considerable amount to juggle, and I learned pretty early on that I wasn't going to be a helicopter mom. I learned that a teenager is no longer a child, and if you want your daughter to be an adult, a fully functioning adult who can make her own decisions and stand on her own two feet, you need to take a step back and let her be responsible for them."

Iris pulled on a pair of hot mitts and opened the oven to lift out a huge pot of shepherd's pie. As she rested it on a hot plate on the island, Jenny wondered if she was planning on feeding everyone.

"So your kids got in trouble, then?" she said.

Iris dragged her gaze over to her, and she thought Karen stifled a laugh. Meanwhile, Suzanne's expression wasn't giving anything away as she turned to her mom, her arms crossed, as if she had decided to just listen and take everything in, then cast judgement.

"Trouble?" Iris blew out a breath, her expression dramatic. She glanced up as if thinking. "Let's see. There was Luke constantly taking off and me having to call the sheriff, and then there was Marcus, who was suspended from school after being caught smoking and cheating on a test—and then there was the graffiti. Pretty sure Ryan was responsible for that one, but he never got caught. He was wily. Add in the court time with Luke after he busted a teacher's nose..."

"Mister Lewis, he was an asshole. He deserved it," Suzanne cut in. "Luke was defending you."

"What? Why?" Iris said.

All Jenny could do was watch the back-and-forth,

seeing that Iris likely didn't know even half of what her kids had done. She wasn't sure if that was supposed to make her feel better.

"Oh, he was kind of a chauvinist, always telling sexist jokes in class. Don't think he liked girls or women. One day he went too far and made a joke about you, said it was unfortunate that Dad had left, as the O'Connells were now known as a bunch of hoodlums because their mom wasn't looking after them as she should be."

Iris just stared, and Suzanne gestured as she continued, glancing over to Jenny. "You see, Mom always insisted we were old enough to step up to the plate. She wasn't going to be waking us up for school. We were old enough to set our own alarms, and if we woke up late and had to race out the door wearing yesterday's clothes, with our hair sticking up, then that was on us. You never had breakfast ready for us, either. We had to make it ourselves if we wanted to eat. I remember you said that your job was to make sure there was food in the house, but it was up to us to pack our own lunches and make ourselves breakfast.

"Then there was the laundry. If we didn't have clean clothes, that was on us, as we were all responsible for doing our own laundry and pitching in. If we forgot something or waited until the very last minute, Mom wasn't going to run out to the store to pick it up for us. If we didn't bring what we needed for a school project and got a zero in class because of it, she said that was just too bad, and if we had to retake the class, then hopefully that would be enough of a lesson for us. Then there was the paperwork from school, all those permission slips and forms that had to be filled out. Mom made us fill them out completely so the only thing she had to do was sign them."

Jenny looked over to their mom, who wore an odd smile and was holding her head high, nodding.

"Karen learned to forge my signature," Iris said, dragging her gaze over to her daughter as if to make a point, teasing.

"Hey, it was just one less thing for you to do, Mom," Karen said.

Jenny was pretty sure Suzanne was trying not to laugh as she said, "Wasn't that for that overnight trip with Gus Littlejohn, because there'd be no chaperones?"

Karen winced. "Tattletale…"

Iris just lifted her gaze to the ceiling. Boy, something about hearing all this had the O'Connell family seeming more human and relatable. "So that's why Luke broke that teacher's nose, because I wouldn't do everything for you?"

Suzanne shrugged. "No, he called me up in the middle of class and made me stand there beside his desk as everyone was working and listening, and he asked me what was wrong with you that you couldn't be more attentive to us and more involved with our academics, monitoring our grades. He said when he called you to say my grades were barely passable, apparently you responded by saying you had no intention of babysitting any of us with school or standing over us like we were six years old. You said we were old enough to understand the importance of doing our homework and passing our classes, and if we failed and had to redo a class or stay later, we would learn pretty quick the consequences of our actions.

"You said you had no time to be following us around and micromanaging our lives, making decisions for us, because we were all teenagers and were learning to be responsible adults, to stand on our own two feet. He said you didn't care about us, that you weren't much of a mother and should be doing more for us. So when Luke saw how upset I was at lunch, I told him everything, and he tracked down Mister Lewis, punched him in the face, and said, 'Don't you ever talk about my mother like that again.'"

Jenny wasn't sure what expression was on her face, but it likely matched the shock on Iris's.

"I didn't know that was what happened," Iris said. "Now I feel horrible, because I grounded him for a month and made him do all that work to cover the cost of the lawyer I had to hire to get him a slap on the wrist instead of time in Juvie. Why didn't he tell me, or you? At least you should have."

Suzanne shrugged. "He made me promise not to, Mom. He was furious, and rightly so. Anyway, look how we turned out: amazing."

Jenny wondered if this was a pep talk to make her feel better about her troubled daughter.

"See? Six kids," Iris said, and they started laughing.

Just then, her cell phone rang, and Ryan's number was on the screen.

"Hi, did you find her?" she said, slipping off the stool and pressing the phone to her ear. Suzanne, Karen, and Iris talked in low voices behind her.

"She's in the park with Ollie. Marcus is already on his way out there."

"I'm coming, Ryan," she said. She thought she heard someone else in the background.

"Thought you'd say that," he replied. "I'll be pulling up in a few minutes to pick you up. Be ready."

She hung up the phone, flooded with relief. This was something Wren would never have done. "That was Ryan," she told the others, gesturing toward the door with her thumb. "They found her. He's picking me up so we can go get her."

"Go," Iris said and started toward her. She set her hand on her shoulder, rubbing, and then hugged her.

"Then, once you're settled," she continued, "I'd like to meet her."

Jenny couldn't explain this feeling of acceptance, and she knew Iris wouldn't care how off the rails her daughter was.

Chapter 18

"She's not here," Marcus said. He was walking their way, shining a flashlight toward them.

The night had settled in as Jenny stood beside Ryan's truck, which was parked in the backwoods lot at the base of the trail. Luke, who'd been in the back seat, stepped around her and placed his hand on her shoulder for a second. Something about being there now with Ryan and his brothers felt surreal. It had from the minute he'd pulled up as she walked out of the house.

"What do you mean, she's not here?" Jenny said. "Ryan, you said you talked to Ollie."

"Yeah, we did," Marcus said. "He's here."

She hadn't seen the gangly teen beside him, whose hands were shoved in the pockets of his baggy jeans. His hair was on the longish side.

"Ah, sorry, I guess you're Alison's mom?" Ollie said.

She kept moving and found herself standing beside Ryan, unsure what to say to this boy. Everything seemed so awkward, and she welcomed the darkness, because it gave her a feeling of anonymity that she couldn't have explained. "I am. So where is my daughter? I understand she was with you. I'd like to know what she's thinking and what she's doing out here, because this is beyond anything I expected—not that I know what to expect anymore."

"Look, she was here," Ollie said, "but she heard me talking to my dad and Deputy O'Connell, and when I told them I was here and she was with me, she got really mad. She said she wasn't waiting around. She was going up to the shelter I showed her, a place we go just to hang out. I tried to stop her and called her, and I was about to go after her when I heard you coming." He was looking at Marcus, and all Jenny could think was to wonder what the hell was going through Alison's head.

She was at a loss for words, but she finally got her tongue to move. "Where did she go? Why is she running? Ryan, what the hell is it with her? I can't believe she'd do this—but at the same time, I can. Like, why is she doing this to me? It's cruel. All I did was try to protect her…"

"I know," he said. "Hey, we'll find her. This isn't all on you. Alison has some responsibility here, too." He had his hand on her shoulder, and she turned to face him and allowed his arm to linger. It felt good. "Look, I'll go after her," he said. "I'll find her."

And she knew he would. She really believed it.

"Where exactly is this shelter, kid?" Luke said.

Jenny was still leaning against Ryan as she turned and took him in. She was touching his arm. She still wanted to wring her daughter's neck.

"At the first mile marker, a fork in the path," Ollie said. "Look, I like Alison. When she showed up at school, she didn't fit in, just like me, so we clicked. She seemed kind of lost and everything. She said you're her dad. She saw you today…" He was pointing at Luke, who was standing right in front of him, arms crossed, looking down at him.

"Yeah, you approached me as I came out of the beer store. She asked me to buy her beer. You follow me or something?"

The kid shrugged. "She knew your name. You were easy to find. We were actually outside your house, and we followed you this afternoon to the liquor store, I didn't expect her to ask you for beer. She said she wanted to just talk to you, but I guess she chickened out."

"Well, he's not her father," Ryan said. "I am. She had the wrong O'Connell."

Jenny stood there, wondering if this was where her daughter had been when she was supposed to be in school. She couldn't shake her feeling of frustration and helplessness.

"I know where that shelter is," Luke said. "Sounds like the one I built way back when, kind of a lean-to under three fir trees…"

Ollie nodded. "Yeah, that's it. Great view. Overlooks the valley."

"She's going to find it in the dark?" Marcus said.

"Look, I know the way up," Ryan said. His hand was still on her arm. "Maybe we can get a search party started, too. If she's lost, she could be just about anywhere. How long ago did she take off?"

"I'm right here."

There was that feeling of surrealness again. It took Jenny a second after hearing the voice that came out of nowhere to realize that it was her daughter.

"Alison?" she said.

Marcus and Ryan shone their flashlights, and there was her daughter, wearing a loose tank top, low cut, and those godawful jean shorts that were so high Jenny knew her butt cheeks were hanging out. She squinted in the light as she walked closer.

"Hey, Alison," Marcus said. "A lot of folks have been worried about you."

Jenny was still taking in her daughter. She couldn't remember ever having seen her look so damn vulnerable. She started over to her and pulled her into her arms. "I am so angry at you," she said. "Why didn't you tell me that your dad had told you he wasn't your father? Running off like this isn't the answer, Alison. And cutting school…" She held her daughter away from her, really looking at her. It was dark out, but the flashlight was behind her. Still, she was having trouble making out what her daughter was thinking or feeling. She felt her shrug.

"I heard you just now," Alison said. "Did you know he was my father?"

Jenny didn't have to look behind her to know she was talking about Ryan, as she could feel him step up behind her.

"It seems we have a lot to talk about, Alison," he said. "But yes, I'm your father, not Luke. I guess I'd like to know a lot of things, but how about we get out of here, and then we can sit down? I have questions, and I'm sure you do, too. We can talk, the three of us, your mom, you, and me."

Her daughter stiffened, and Jenny could feel her anger. "He didn't know about you, Alison," she said. "I didn't tell Ryan. There was no reason to. I was already with your dad. We got married, and he wanted to be your father— but at the same time, I didn't know Wren told you. He never wanted you to know. I know things got bad, and what happened…"

Alison said nothing. Jenny knew there was so much more that her daughter knew and she didn't. She could feel everyone watching, listening.

Then Ryan somehow maneuvered her and Alison into

his pickup, and he climbed behind the wheel and simply said, "Luke's riding with Marcus."

When he started the truck, she didn't miss the way he glanced in the rear-view mirror at Alison in the back seat. Instead of saying anything else, he put the truck in gear and just drove.

Chapter 19

Ryan felt a sense of urgency he never had before as he drove in silence with the woman who'd haunted him since that night together so long ago, and the girl in the back seat who appeared to sulk in silence. He tried to see some of himself in her, a resemblance through the painted face, the hair dye, through everything she seemed to be trying to change about herself.

He could feel her hurt, pain, trauma as he drove in the darkness down their street, and still no one had said a word as he pulled up and parked in the driveway in front of his house, beside hers.

He turned off the truck and stepped out just as Alison and Jenny did. "We're talking now, at my house," he said and gestured to the darkened windows. Both just stared at him. He couldn't have explained to anyone why he needed to control his turf.

"I want to take a shower," Alison said, then shut the door and started walking around the truck to her house. She wasn't about to make any of this easy. Jenny sighed from where she stood on the other side of the truck, and she didn't have to say a word.

"Hey!" Ryan called out. "Stop walking right now."

But Alison was already across the brown grass to her house and heading up the stairs. He started after her, and Jenny fell in beside him.

"See what I'm up against?" she said. "It's not you, Ryan. She's just not going to go quietly and listen."

"She needs some ground rules…"

"You see how well that's worked so far? Or is this where you try to say that because you're her father, a man, you can get her to listen more than I can?"

That was the reality of it, but he hadn't expected her to say so. Jenny followed Alison inside, where the lights were already on, and Ryan felt himself drowning. How had his mom ever done it with six of them? They hadn't made it easy, either. He was sensing the impossibility of it as he followed Jenny inside. Alison was already on the staircase.

"Hey, stop!" His voice was loud, and the demand was clear.

He expected her to keep going, to ignore him, but she stopped, and for a second he could see how rattled she was, maybe at his tone.

He walked over to the staircase and rested his hand on the rail. "You can shower after, but we're talking first. Come on down here," he said, staying right where he was.

She stood there, as in a standoff.

When he took in her indecency, the little she was wearing, it was on the tip of his tongue to ask her to change. Instead he said, "Your mom told me what happened in Atlanta, the shooting…"

He wasn't sure what to make of her expression. She was just a kid trying to be an adult and failing miserably.

"Come on down here now," he continued and gestured

toward her, the same motion he used with troublemakers in the park, and he couldn't have explained his relief as she walked back down, though dragging her heels.

He gestured to the living room, where he'd sat more than a few times while Althea served him tea and something freshly baked from the oven. He allowed his gaze to slide over to Jenny, who was watching her daughter, watching him, as if she expected this to be a trick or for something to go completely haywire.

"Is it true?" Alison said, like an accusation.

"Yes. I told Ryan what happened."

"No, about him being my father." She jabbed her arm toward him as if he were no one, and she sounded furious, as if him being her father was the worst thing possible.

Jenny strode into the living room and took a seat in one of the easy chairs, and Alison took up a spot by the window, standing. Was there anything of him in her face? She had Jenny's brown eyes, those amazing big brown pools, but her mouth and the way she held it so stubbornly seemed so much like an O'Connell.

"Yes, Ryan is your biological father," Jenny said.

"Why would you hide it?"

It seemed Alison operated from only two emotions, anger and resentment, but Jenny sat so calmly in the chair, tapping her fingers on the arm as if considering what to say. Ryan knew there was so much more about her that he didn't know.

"I met your dad…" she started.

"Wren isn't my dad!" Alison said, cutting her off, and Ryan realized she also had only two ways of talking to her mom, either yelling at her or ignoring her.

"Do you not want to know, Alison?" Jenny said. "Because I'm getting really tired of the way you're talking to me as if you hate me. Enough, already. Sit your ass down over there and listen for once in your life. This anger you have for me, I'm done with it. Everything I've done has been for you, so I'm just asking for a little give here, Alison. You want answers? Then sit down and shut the hell up and just listen!" She pulled in a breath as if she'd run a marathon, and Ryan could feel her anger, how unsettled she was.

"Look, let's all calm down," he said. "Alison, sit down. Jenny…" He strode over to the sofa, gesturing to it.

Alison wrapped both her hands around herself, tapping her foot, the anger rooting her to her spot. He could see her considering something, ready to race out, to vent. Then she sat down, and for a second he wanted to let out a sigh of relief. Had he seriously been thinking it would be easy?

"Your mom is trying to tell you that she was with your dad when she found out she was pregnant with you," he said. "They were already building a life together. Your mom and I were together only once." He leveled a glance at Jenny, signaling for her to continue.

"That's right," she said. "There was no reason to tell Ryan. I was already in Atlanta with Wren. I had met him shortly after Ryan, and we were in love. He said it didn't matter. He'd be your father. That was the way he wanted it. We got married, and he loved you, and he was a father to you. Ryan never knew about you."

Alison was sitting stiffly, still tapping her foot, anger ricocheting through her. She was looking over to her mom and to him, and he took in the exasperation on Jenny's face.

"That's right," he said. "I didn't know. I just found out, and I'm still in shock, but I can also tell you, Alison, I'm not washing my hands of you. You're my kid, which means we're in each other's lives whether you like it or not. I'm not going anywhere. I would have wanted you if I'd known about you, but here we are. We can't go backwards, and I'm not turning my back on you. At the same time, when you pull crap like this and take off and do stupid-ass things, thinking you can do and say whatever you want and hurt anyone because you're hurting…I'm here to tell you that it stops, Alison. No more." He sat down on the arm of the sofa and didn't pull his gaze from his daughter. He wondered how long he'd have to wait until she decided to give just a bit.

"Yeah, so you think you get to suddenly tell me what to do?" she said. "Step in like a dad and be a dad to me? What if I tell you I don't want you in my life? I don't want to know you."

He got the bite. It was cruel, how she spoke, and he had to remind himself this was just a scared kid lashing out. "Then I'd tell you too bad, because I'm not going anywhere. All that aside, though, we have a bigger problem. Wren told you he wasn't your dad, so why is it that you thought my brother Luke was your father? In your journal, what you wrote…"

The look she gave him revealed her betrayal, and she leveled a glare at Jenny. "You read my journal?"

"I read it," Ryan said, "with my brother Marcus. You were missing, so yeah, you bet we went through everything of yours to find you. What I don't understand is why you thought it was Luke, why you took off the way you did, why you approached him and tried to hustle beer. Where did you get these answers from? I have to wonder if there's more I don't know. Alison, look, you need to level with us. You're in trouble, and unless you talk, I don't know how to help." He was leaning forward, pleading. Did other parents do this as well? It was such a helpless place to be.

Alison just shrugged.

"Alison, I never knew your dad told you that you weren't his," Jenny said. "That was cruel. He never wanted you to know, so I'm at a loss as to why he'd do it. Why did he say what he did to you? Why did you shoot your father?"

Time slowed. Alison lifted her gaze to her mom so sharply, and her expression changed from anger to confusion. "I didn't shoot Dad," she said, her voice so low.

He found himself leaning forward, and it took him another second to realize she was probably in shock, blocking it out.

She shook her head and looked over to him, and it was there in her eyes, in her expression. She had changed from a kid who thought she knew everything to a scared little girl. "I didn't do it," she said. "I was hurt and angry at him for ripping my world apart. One minute I thought he was my dad, and then he wasn't. I tried to protect you, Mom. After one of those fights, he was so cruel to you. The way he talked to you, and you let him… I told him to stop, and he said that he and I were so much alike, and the sad part was that I wasn't even his. He said I'd never be like you, Mom, and he said thank God for that.

"It was later that same night. He was drinking like he always did, and I went back downstairs to confront him and demand he take back the lie, but on the way down, I heard the gunshot and saw a man run out of the house. I ran into his office and found him lying there, bleeding. He said he was sorry for everything he did to me, for telling me he wasn't my father, for a lot of things. I screamed at him and asked who my father was, my real father, and he said he was in Livingston. He kept saying 'O'Connell.' He had a file on him, everything about him. I knew Dad had files in the drawer in his office, in the cabinet, where he kept secrets about people.

"I just saw the gun on the ground, and I walked over and picked it up. Then you ran in, Mom, and I froze, I just froze, because I didn't know what to do. Then I just left and ran…" She was crying, her forearm over her face.

"Hey, hey, it's okay," Jenny said. She hurried over and sat beside Alison on the sofa, and Ryan moved right in front of her, looking down, taking in the shock on Jenny's face. She had completely misunderstood what had happened. "I thought you shot your dad," she said. "You were holding the gun, and you didn't say anything."

Alison was shaking her head, still crying, sniffing. When she dropped her arm, he could see her shaking. Her eyes were red, and the thick black liner and mascara was a mess.

As he leaned down and touched her shoulder, he just took in this girl who was his, seeing what she was doing to her body, how she looked, and he sat on the sofa table in front of her, right in front of Jenny, so close his knees were bumping theirs.

"Hey," he said. "I don't want you to worry about this. I'm going to take care of it. We're going to fix it. Do you know who it was who shot your dad?" He didn't allow his gaze to linger too long on Jenny as he took in his daughter, who now suddenly seemed so young.

"He worked for Dad," she said. "That guy with the glasses. He always wore suits, the same ones, blue and black…Troy Johnson. Is that all? Because I want a shower, and I don't want to talk about this anymore."

"Yeah, of course, go shower," Jenny said even though he wanted to keep her talking and question her and find out everything. But he said nothing as he watched Alison walk away and up the stairs, hearing her footsteps, then a door closing.

He gave everything to Jenny, who was doing her best to

hold it all together, but it was hard when her world had been so suddenly and completely rocked.

"Oh my God, Ryan…" She lifted her gaze to his, struggling for words. "I thought it was her who shot him. I hid the gun."

He sat up and rested his hands on his knees, taking in the house around them, hearing the shower upstairs, knowing all too well that tampering with evidence at a crime scene was as bad as it could get.

"First things first, I need you to tell me everything," he said. "Everything you did from the minute you hid the gun —and I want to know everything that happened between you and Wren."

She pulled in a breath and looked away for a second. "Where do you want me to start?" she finally said, and for the first time, he thought he was actually reaching her.

"At the beginning."

Chapter 20

She couldn't remember the last time she'd heard her daughter laugh. It had been so long that the sound of her laughter and the teasing of family coming from her living room had Jenny pausing, knife in hand, as she chopped up carrots for a veggie tray.

She stood for a second, just listening to the voices and the joy as she thought of everything that had happened in the past few days. All of it had felt like a bad dream, but now, for the first time she could remember, she felt as if her life and her daughter's were on the right trajectory.

Everything in the house that had belonged to Wren was in a storage unit in her name, including the grease trap with the gun. She still couldn't believe she'd covered up a crime for someone else. The horror of what she'd done and the reality of the trouble she could be in had kept her awake that first night. At the same time, she knew who Troy was, and she knew Wren had likely dug up something on him. She hadn't even known where to begin to fix it.

Ryan had called Marcus.

Marcus had called the Atlanta PD.

Meanwhile, Luke had sat and listened, and Karen had told her to say nothing. Suzanne and Owen had said that family looked after family, and Iris had simply told Ryan and Marcus to take care of it.

What that meant, she didn't know. For the first time in her life, she felt as if she were part of something bigger, and there were people who had her and her daughter's backs.

Then there was her life with Wren, the depravity of what he'd demanded of her, the nights he'd hurt her because he could. Ryan had just listened, but she hadn't told him everything. There were just some things that went on between a man and his wife, sexually, that she couldn't talk about—the pleasure, the pain, and how Wren had got off on it.

Maybe Ryan knew. Maybe that was why he still slept next door, at his house, but spent the rest of his time at hers.

"Mom, come here! He's on the news," Alison called out.

She heard the squeak of the steps as Ryan entered the house. Luke was perched on the sofa, beer in hand, Karen was in a chair with a glass of wine, and Suzanne was digging in the artichoke dip on the table. Iris was standing just off to the side.

Everyone was looking at the TV, at a CNN broadcast from Atlanta, where Troy Johnson was in cuffs.

"They arrested him for Dad's murder…" Alison said.

Jenny took in her daughter, who was wearing a pair of blue jeans and a short crop top that showed off a belly piercing. Her face was free of the makeup that had become part of who she was, and her hair was now her natural shade of brown. She thought she had Iris to thank for that. Alison's grandmother seemed to know how to talk to her daughter, how to get her to do something and make her think it had been her idea.

Ryan's hand rested on her shoulder and then the small of her back. She looked up at him, still hearing the sound of the TV.

"How? I don't understand…" she said.

Marcus was there too, on the other side of Ryan. Just something about them told her they were behind this, but how?

"We just righted a wrong, is all," he said. "Made sure the case was closed and no questions could come your way or Alison's."

She just stared at both of them, not understanding what they'd done. She knew the three brothers had gone to Atlanta late the previous afternoon and had come back just that day. "I want to know…" she started.

Marcus and Ryan exchanged a look, then glanced over to Luke, who had flicked the remote to turn the game back on, Penn State against Tennessee. Marcus said not a word as he walked over to the rest of the family, where he set his hand on Alison's head and rustled her hair. She smiled, and Jenny was again stuck on this instant family, how they'd come together for them, how each of them had connected with Alison—the kid, as they all called her.

"There's one less thing in your storage locker," Ryan said. "Marcus found out that the Atlanta PD had a file on you and Alison and no other leads, but your husband had files on a lot of people, important people."

"But how…? I don't understand."

It was the way he looked at her, the way she stood beside him, so close. He had made not one move to kiss her, just gave her a simple touch here and there. He reached for her hand and pulled her outside on the porch so they were alone. She took in her Jeep in the driveway, the rusty Hyundai she still needed to sell, and the other cars and trucks of Ryan's family, who, it seemed, were always there.

"I said I would handle it, and we did," he said. "I know what you told me about Wren, what he did, how he treated you. I'm not like that, Jenny. I would never do that to you, keep something from you, hide the kind of secrets he did, control you the way he did. We found a way to right history, to change the outcome, to get the smoking gun where it needed to be. So when I say all this, know that I'm not telling you how to think or telling you that you don't need to know. I'm just saying it's been taken care of. Troy's going to jail. The case is being closed. And I want you and Alison to move in with me."

For a minute, she wasn't sure she'd heard him correctly. He stepped forward and set his hands on her shoulders, ran them down her arms, and rested them on her hips, over her jean shorts. She stood barefoot on the front porch, staring at a man she felt as if she'd known a lifetime, yet it had been only a few days since he'd first walked back into her life.

"You want me and Alison to move in with you?"

He angled his head, standing so close to her, his hands sliding over the small of her back. "Yes."

"As roommates?" she said, feeling foolish, and took in the odd smile on his face.

"No, not as roommates. I want to get to know my daughter, and you. You know, you've never told me why you slipped away that night without a word. It may have been just sex, but there was something about it. I never got you out of my mind. I wanted something more then."

He was still holding her, and she remembered all too well that night, the passion. She'd seen him across the bar and made her way over, not expecting the night to turn out as it had.

"All I can say is I left because I didn't want to hear you tell me to get lost, you know, the same old lines, like 'This has been fun. I'll call you,' and then I never hear from you. So I did the only thing I could think of to feel in control, like I was leaving with dignity…" She shrugged.

For a second, she wondered what would have happened if she'd stayed, the life she and Alison would have had, how different it would have been. "But we can't go back, Ryan," she finally said. "We only have right now. We only have this moment to go forward—and no, I don't want to move in with you over there. This is my house that my aunt left me, and it's the first time I've had something that's all mine."

"I really get that, Jenny, but this neighbor thing isn't going to work, with me living next door to you," he said. Then he leaned down and kissed her. Her hands pressed into his chest, fisting his shirt. He pulled back. "But if you want to take it slow, I can do that."

This was something else she hadn't expected.

"I like your mom, Ryan," she said. "But what happened to your dad? None of you talk about him."

He said nothing at first. She could feel something in him seem to pull back. She wasn't sure what it was. "He left," he said, then shrugged and glanced out into the darkness. "He was just gone one day."

"So you've never heard from him?"

"He made a choice to leave. Nope, never heard from him. I know Luke tried to find him once. Not sure if he did. We never talked about it."

"And you didn't?"

What was it about this man? She sensed he was holding on to his own pain.

He shook his head. "No, I don't want to know. He left, never reached out. Kind of says everything. Besides, this is about you and me. I don't want to rush you, but at the same time, Jenny, I mean it when I say I'm not Wren."

The way he said it scared the hell out of her, because she knew it was true.

"I need to be sure this time," she said, thinking of Alison inside and this man standing in front of her. It seemed too good to be true.

"Then take as long as you need, but until then, you'd better get used to having me around," he said, then pulled her closer, and she settled her arms over his shoulders, feeling his strength, his height.

"I guess I can handle that."

When he leaned in and kissed her again, for the first time, she felt as if something in her life could turn out all right.

Chapter 21

"So you're heading off. Can you tell us where you're going this time?" Marcus said from where he lingered outside.

"Or how long you'll be gone?" Ryan added, already missing his brother.

Luke stepped out onto Jenny's front porch and let the screen door close behind him. After another family night, Luke was now being shipped off. Ryan could hear Jenny inside with his sisters, his mom, and a daughter he was doing his best to get to know. She was circling him cautiously more than talking to him, but he could sense her need to open up.

One day at a time, his mom had said.

"You know better," Luke replied. "Can't say. Well, I'll see you on the flip side. It'll take as long as it takes."

Ryan knew that was Luke's way of saying it was classified. It could be weeks or months before he was back stateside from some part of the world the average person didn't know about. He wanted to tell him to stay safe, to come back alive, to not dare fucking die. But he didn't.

Instead, he said, "I'm going to say it even though I know you don't want to hear it. Thank you for what you did for my kid, and for Jenny."

Luke said nothing. Ryan could tell he was uncomfortable. It was him who'd taken the gun from the grease trap and said he'd make sure it was found where it should be. Ryan didn't know how he'd gotten into Troy's house or where he'd planted the gun, and he didn't need to know. Luke was good at what he did.

"Told you to knock it off and stop worrying. Nothing will come back on her. The gun was clean of prints, but ballistics will show it's a match. It'll look as if he cleaned the gun and stashed it. So how did Atlanta PD get the tip?" Luke said, though he was looking right at Marcus, and something passed between them.

"That's the thing about anonymous tips," Marcus said. "They're anonymous. It's all good, Ryan. Don't worry. We did it for that kid in there. After all, she's family. So you're really moving in here with Jenny?"

"Eventually," Ryan said. "We'll get there. She wants to take it slow. I guess I can give her that."

Then he hugged his brother in that brotherly way he always did before he shipped out, and he watched him walk away and climb behind the wheel of the pickup truck.

"Stop worrying about him," Marcus said. "He'll be fine."

They watched their brother start to pull away, and Marcus lingered beside him. He was wearing blue jeans and a faded striped T-shirt, a beer in his hand. Just then, Owen pulled up in his plumbing van and honked, and Luke paused. Owen hopped out and went to the window, evidently to say his own goodbye.

"I know," Ryan said. "It's just hard, you know. We never know where he's going or if he's coming home."

Marcus rested his hand on his shoulder and squeezed. "Can I get you another beer?" he finally said, and he headed into the house.

Owen started up the steps, ballcap on backwards, jeans ripped at the knees. It would be another night of the family together. "So who won the game?" he said as they walked into the house.

"No idea," Ryan replied. Inside, he took in his sisters and mom in the kitchen with Alison, where everyone had gathered, feeling their family together in a way he couldn't explain.

Then there was Jenny. Something about her smile told him that she fit in. Judging by her laugh, how relaxed she was, maybe there could really be some kind of future for them.

One day at a time, though.

Then, just maybe, everything would be perfect.

Chapter 22

As Ryan blinked in the early morning light, it took him a second to realize where he was, feeling the sexy, gorgeous woman in bed beside him, her warmth pressed against him. The sheets were twisted around him and Jenny, and he heard nothing but the quiet of the morning, seeing on the bedside clock that it was just past six.

He pressed a kiss to her shoulder, and she murmured softly. He wanted to remind her that they needed to get up soon, as he had work, and so did she. Then there was their kid in the house, who wasn't exactly a well-adjusted teen thrilled with her current lot in life.

But he wanted to lie like this for another moment before he rolled her over, touched her, and made love to her again. He planned on it, considering he felt that was the perfect way to wake up in the morning.

They had taken it slow because that had been what she wanted, even though Ryan considered sleeping together to be at the top of the list in terms of getting to know someone and building the perfect well-balanced relationship, with talking, sharing, and being together.

He kissed her neck and allowed his hand to trail over the flat of her stomach and the swell of her breasts, and she moaned softly. He felt her beginning to stir, to stretch, before she rolled over and allowed him to settle once again on top of her, to slip inside her, to love her again.

Her hands were in his hair around him, pulling him closer, when he heard a loud crash downstairs as if something heavy had been dropped, and he froze, pulling back and staring at the closed white bedroom door. Jenny stiffened under him.

"She's up," he said.

Jenny shut her eyes and sighed in that way of hers, as if giving herself a mental pep talk to go and deal with her daughter. She pressed her hand to her forehead, brushing back her hair, and he slid off her and sat at the edge of the bed, hearing the creak of the metal frame. As he put his bare feet on the floor, he allowed the sheet to fall away.

"She is," Jenny said. "She knows you stayed over, or she wants something, or…"

"I'll go and talk to her," he said. This was all so new, staying over but keeping his house next door, sneaking out in the early morning before Alison was up so he could go home and shower and change. They were still in the "taking it slow" stage—not him, but her.

He knew why, because of the demons she still carried from having been married to a man like Wren. How could she have loved a man who could manipulate her the way Wren had? The idea of it still had him wondering where her head was, and he thought that was why he was still having to leave at dawn.

He kept his house, and she kept hers.

He stood up naked, feeling the cool air, and reached for

his pants on the floor in a heap with Jenny's shirt and sweats from the night before. It seemed that was the one thing they were doing really well, having sex and sleeping, not so much talking and relating. She was as closed as her daughter.

He zipped up his fly and reached for his white T-shirt on the floor. Jenny had propped herself up on her elbow, and the sheet just covered those remarkable breasts. She watched him unabashedly as he pulled his shirt over his head.

"You know she knows you're here," she said, her voice so soft. She didn't look like the mother of a teenager, and he was certainly still trying to wrap his head around the fact that he had a kid. He was now a father to a girl who made nothing easy.

"I know, which is why I'll go down and deal with her," he said, then heard a loud clunk again that sounded like it came from the kitchen. She was really banging things around.

Jenny winced. "You'd better hurry before she takes my kitchen down around us or breaks something that really does matter to me." She lay back down on the mattress, pressing her head into the pillow, the sheet covering her again.

He pulled open the door and stepped out barefoot before pulling it closed behind him, then went down the stairs, running his hand over his thick hair and yawning. The stairs creaked, and the noise from the kitchen suddenly stopped.

He took in the locked front door, the way the early morning light filled the living room, the white walls covered in old photos and artwork, and he walked down the hall to the kitchen. The first thing he saw were Alison's deep brown eyes staring back at him. Her mouth was tight and frowning, and she stood on the other side of the island. Her hair was short, freshly cut, and he thought his sister Karen, or maybe Suzanne, was responsible for the new neat and tidy look.

"Good morning, sunshine," he said. "You're sure the early riser today. Heard your wake-up call. Did you start the coffee?"

He wasn't sure what to make of her expression. She was guarded, on edge, and she moved around the island in a short nightshirt that stopped just above her knees. He took in the carton of milk, the frying pan, a jug of water, and two large mixing bowls on the island, evidently the source of the banging.

"You making breakfast for us?" he said. He just couldn't help himself.

She was still acting from that angry, hurt, and frustrated place. He took in the carafe, which was cold and empty, and pulled it out and rinsed it under the tap, then filled it with water, very aware she still hadn't answered him.

"Where does your mom keep the coffee?" he asked, pouring the cold water in the reservoir and then lifting out the basket of yesterday's grounds, which he dumped in the garbage under the sink. When he looked over at Alison, the frown was still on her face, and she had moved so the island was between them.

"So are you living here now?" she said, cutting right through the bullshit.

"Sounds to me like you have some issues with that," he said. He rinsed the basket and tossed it back in. "You want to talk about it?"

She just shrugged and then pointed to the cupboard in front of him. Evidently not. "Coffee and filters," she said. She really didn't say a lot when she didn't want to, and her personality had an edge to it, rough, frayed, and jagged.

"Thanks," he said as he dumped the filter and coffee into the basket and pressed the button to start the brew. When he turned and leaned against the counter, she was eyeing him up like a wary dog who was just waiting to be kicked and would attack and bite before he could take a single step.

"You're having sex with my mom," she said.

If he'd been drinking coffee, he'd have spit it out.

"You're just a kid," he replied. "You shouldn't be talking like that."

But then, considering what she'd seen and done, she really wasn't a typical fourteen-year-old, whose only worries were homework and school dances and when her favorite show was on TV.

"So what should I be saying—fucking, screwing? What are you doing with my mom?" What do you want from her? Are you toying with her, messing with her, fucking with her, trying to hurt her? Are you playing a game of some kind?" Her expression told him there was something more to her questions.

"Whoa, Alison, what's going on?" he said. "You, me, and your mom are trying to build something here. I thought we talked about this. Are you telling me you don't want me here?"

For a second, he didn't think he should have put that out there, because he might not like her answer, and he had no intention of letting her push him away.

But then she shrugged. "I want to know what my mom means to you. Is she just someone for you to have fun with, toy with, hurt…?"

There it was. How much of the sick relationship between Wren and Jenny did she know about? He suspected more than a kid should. Jenny had been vague, but she'd said enough that he knew the man liked it rough.

"I wouldn't be here if I wanted fun," he replied. "I told your mom I want something more, and I would never hurt her or you. Besides, your mom's already put the brakes on. If I had my way, we'd all be living under one roof now—my roof. As it is, I'm having to tread carefully until she's comfortable. You're not without a voice here either, Alison, but you're my kid, which means we're in each other's lives forever regardless of whether your mom and I have a relationship. By the way, though, yes, your mom and I are involved. I care about her very much, and you."

For a minute, he wasn't sure what she was going to say. If anything, she seemed uncomfortable, hesitant.

"So you don't have another girlfriend or someone else you're taking out, sleeping around with?" she said. "You're always here, yet you keep your house next door, kind of like you want the best of both worlds. You have your space, and where does that leave us?"

The coffeemaker beeped. He knew his mouth was open in shock, so he reached behind him and pulled out a mug, then poured himself a coffee, wondering what she was getting at. "First, I don't have a girlfriend or, as you so directly put it, another woman I'm sleeping with. I'm single, or I was, but now I'm not. I wouldn't be here with you and your mom if I was seeing someone. Told you before that your mom and I are trying to build something, a relationship. Your mom wants to take it slow, which is the only reason I've been leaving at dawn to my house. We'll get there, though, and figure it out, and when everyone is comfortable, you and your mom, both of you…" He gestured with his coffee mug. "Then either you'll move over to my place, or…" He would have to move in here.

"Then there's you and me. Aren't you back to school today?"

After she had been kicked out of so many classes, he and Jenny had had to smooth out the problems and talk the principal into giving her another chance, and today was the day.

"I don't feel well," she said and forced a pathetic cough.

He just stared at her, and she stared right back at him. "Really," he said. "You sound fine to me. You know, it's not going to get easier, avoiding this. School should be fun. Just go and stop putting it off."

He could vaguely hear his phone ringing from upstairs in the bedroom, and then he thought he heard Jenny answering it. He found himself looking up at the ceiling, hearing the squeak of the old floorboards. Evidently, she was up. He could hear her footsteps on the stairs.

"Fun for who? I told you, I'm sick." Alison forced a cough again.

Jenny was still talking as she made her way down to them. He wondered what his own mom would have said to him in this situation. Probably just told him to get his ass in gear and get to school.

"Listen, you have only one job, and that's to be a kid and go to school," he said. "Your mom and I have already talked to the principal, and you now have a second chance, so how about meeting us halfway?"

"He's right here," Jenny said. She was behind him now, and he took in her long floral robe, her hair a tousled mess. She held out his cell phone to him. "It's your sister."

He took the phone before he could ask which one. "Hey," was all he said as he pressed it to his ear. Behind him, he heard Jenny telling Alison to get ready for school and then asking if she'd had breakfast.

"Ryan, have you talked to Marcus yet?" It was Karen.

He turned around, staring out the small kitchen window, seeing his house right next door. He set his coffee on the counter. "No, it's like the crack of dawn. Does no one sleep in?" he said.

Alison said something to Jenny, but he was only half listening, as he thought he heard a vehicle outside.

"Well, we kind of have a problem," Karen said. "You know the storage locker Jenny still has in Atlanta? I told her to empty it and get rid of everything, and she said she would get around to it."

He knew it was something she had been planning. Unfortunately, it was just one more thing she was dragging her feet on, and he had a sinking feeling he wasn't going to like what Karen said next.

"Sure," he said. "Why are you asking about the storage unit?"

When he turned, Jenny was looking at him with wide eyes. He had her attention, and even though it appeared Alison was completely ignoring him, he knew she was listening to everything he was saying, too.

"All I know is that Troy Johnson is out on bail, and questions are being asked about where Wren's belongings ended up. They know about the storage locker, and the defense is pushing someone in the justice department for a warrant to get access to everything in there."

He pressed his fingers to the bridge of his nose and shut his eyes. This was supposed to have been open and shut. He heard the doorbell ring, then a knock on the door, and Jenny started toward it.

"Of course, he's trying to get out of it," he said. "He knew Alison was there, and Jenny, so he's trying to point the finger." He blew out a breath and took in the furrowed line across his daughter's brow. Then he heard Marcus's voice. "Well, looks like Marcus is here."

"Good, then pack a bag," Karen said, "because you're going to Atlanta. You make sure there's nothing in that locker that could lead to Jenny or Alison. Ryan, I know I don't need to tell you this, but if they send in a crime scene team to go through the locker and they find even a sliver of something that could link to the gun, it could allow them to question Troy Johnson's guilt and shine the spotlight elsewhere. You know it's not about who really did it; it's about the story and about having the right kind of evidence."

Marcus was right beside him now, dressed casually in blue jeans and a faded green T-shirt, shades resting in his thick dark hair. Both Jenny and Alison were giving them their full attention.

"Okay, got it," Ryan said, then hung up and dumped his cell phone on the island.

"So you heard," Marcus said, not pulling his gaze from him.

"Do they have a warrant yet?" he asked.

"Not yet, but we expect it," Marcus said. "So pack an overnight bag. We need to go to the airport and catch the next flight out."

"Okay, someone please explain what the hell is going on," Jenny finally cut in, her voice and expression panicked, and he thought Alison had stopped breathing beside her. Ryan didn't pull his gaze from his daughter.

"We need to take care of the locker," Marcus stressed. "We don't know what else is in there, Jenny. Troy's lawyer is really good and is working at getting him off, and it appears that in doing so, he's trying to shift the focus any way he can."

"But you took care of the…" Jenny stopped, and Ryan cleared his throat.

"Yup, but there was a lot of other stuff in there, a lot of boxes," Marcus said. "They found the gun at Troy's, but if there's anything else incriminating, that could suddenly become a problem."

Ryan exhaled, seeing the panic on Jenny's face and the way she pulled in a breath. "Yeah, guess we're going to Atlanta," he said, then reached for his phone and started around the island. "Let me go grab my things."

"Just a second," Jenny said. "Do you think your mom would watch Alison?"

He took in his kid, who still hadn't said anything. "I'm sure, but why?"

Jenny firmed her lips and then nodded, shoving her hands in the pockets of her housecoat. "Because this time, I'm coming too."

Chapter 23

Not only had Iris pulled up in front of the house less than ten minutes after Ryan called her, but she had also insisted that today was not the day her granddaughter was going back to school. She said Alison needed a fun day, and they were going to head off to meet Suzanne, who apparently also had the day off, for an afternoon of pampering, a mani-pedi, lunch, shopping, and whatever else they could think of.

Ryan had argued that Alison needed to go to school and his mom was only enabling her avoidance, but he had evidently changed his mind after seeing his daughter's face when Iris slipped her arm around her shoulder. Iris just seemed to have a way with Alison that no one else did. Well, at least Alison had someone she liked.

After Ryan had tossed his bag in Marcus's pickup, he'd pulled Alison aside, and whatever he'd said to her had her relaxing just a bit. There was something about watching this relationship between father and daughter, something so new. Jenny could see that her daughter was really struggling not to like him.

It was promising.

She felt watchful still as she sat between Ryan and Marcus in a tight coach seat on their last-minute flight to Atlanta. Ryan's hand rested on her thigh, and she leaned against his arm, still considering the question Marcus had insisted on asking. *Is there anything in that locker that could have the authorities looking at either of you?*

She had said nothing. That fact of the matter was that she had packed up all of his files and belongings without a second thought, not wanting to deal with it. She had even given away most of his personal things, and everything that was left was now in storage. She hadn't looked at anything too closely because she hadn't wanted to know. Her one and only priority had been her daughter and moving to Livingston and leaving all this behind.

"You okay?" Ryan said. "You've been pretty quiet since we left."

Marcus was beside her, scrolling through his phone, and didn't seem to be paying any attention to them. She felt Ryan run his hand over her thigh, over her blue jeans. She wore a simple white sleeveless blouse, and her dark hair was pulled back in a ponytail, her face free of makeup. All she had packed in her carry-on was a change of underwear, her deodorant, a toothbrush, and a second sleeveless blouse just in case they didn't make it back that night.

"What can I say? My daughter seems to prefer being with your mom and your sisters over me," she replied. She knew she shouldn't take it personally, but it just added to the uncertainty and worry she was feeling over the kinds of things they'd find in that locker she'd never taken the time to go through.

"It's a phase," Marcus said, jumping in. She hadn't even known he was listening. "Every kid prefers their grandparents or someone who spoils them and lets them have fun, let loose. Just consider it our mom's way of getting back at Ryan."

Ryan only grunted. "She did say she couldn't wait until we had kids so she could enjoy every moment of watching them give us the gears while she stepped in to be the fun one. Apparently, Mom's being true to her word."

"It's payback, Jenny, but just be glad Alison has that."

She wasn't sure what to say to that. "So how much trouble were you for your mom?"

Marcus stared at his phone and laughed under his breath, then glanced her way and over to Ryan, shaking his head. "Oh, we were pretty bad."

"Speak for yourself," Ryan said. "I wasn't as bad as Luke, and then there was Karen."

"Don't forget Suzanne, either. Mom just didn't know all the trouble she got in. And Owen, I swear he's done things none of us know about."

Jenny didn't know what to say.

Just then, the captain announced for them to fasten their seatbelts and prepare for landing. It was a quick arrival and a quick exit off the plane after grabbing their overhead bags. She held Ryan's hand while they made their way through the airport, having to really work to keep up with the brothers' long strides.

Marcus had rented a car, and she found herself tucked in the back seat of the small compact, taking in the back-and-forth between Ryan and Marcus without really listening to what they were saying. As they moved through the afternoon freeway traffic of a city that had once been home, she felt no connection to it now.

"Did you hear me, Jenny?" Ryan called out, looking over his shoulder at her from the passenger side.

"Sorry?" She leaned forward as far as the shoulder strap would allow.

"Marcus has ordered a truck to take the furniture from the locker and give it to charity. Everything else, we'll go through it quickly and get rid of it. I know I asked you before, but is there anything in there you want to keep?"

His eyes were blue as he lifted his sunglasses, surrounded by tiny lines and freckles from the elements. He was so good looking. She pulled in a breath as the big sign for the storage units emerged in the distance. She had been there only once.

"I want nothing," she said.

Ryan was quiet for a second, and she wasn't sure what to make of the way he looked at her. She still hadn't shared everything of what Wren had done, what he'd done to her, what she'd allowed him to do.

He only nodded as Marcus pulled off the freeway. "You hear anything more about if the Atlanta PD got a warrant?" he asked.

Marcus pulled up to the locked gate. "Nothing yet, but then, I may not hear anything until they're on their way."

Maybe that was why she suddenly had a sick feeling in the pit of her stomach. Ryan climbed out, punched in the code she'd given him, and climbed back in as the gate swung open. As Marcus drove in, she could feel her heart hammering, her palms sweating.

He pulled around the corner, and when she saw nothing, she let out a breath that sounded like relief even to her own ears.

They pulled up and parked in front of the storage unit, and they all climbed out. As Ryan unlocked the padlock, she couldn't have explained to anyone the sense of panic and urgency she was feeling. He lifted the door and stepped inside the eight-by-ten space, and the light flicked on.

Jenny took in the concrete walls, the artwork in the

corner, the desk and small furniture she hadn't disposed of. It was considerable. She couldn't help where her gaze landed, on the small cabinet stacked on a side table, where the grease trap had once been. She reached for the handle and pulled it open, and seeing the empty spot had her breathing another sigh of relief.

She felt a hand rest on her shoulder. Ryan was there.

"We need to move quickly," he said. "Let's look through the files and start getting rid of stuff now."

She moved to a stack of taped-up boxes on which she'd scribbled Wren's name in Sharpie. Right, his files, the contents of his desk. She'd simply dumped in all the papers.

As Ryan cut open the first box, she heard a truck and turned sharply. Marcus had just stepped out of the unit to investigate when a guy pulled up with a cube van and parked. It was only the furniture truck.

She gave everything to the files in the box, seeing names of who she knew were important people. Everything Wren had done left her feeling as if the man she'd married had been a stranger. There was also a small locked box that she'd forgotten about. It had been in the bottom of his desk, and she'd never found the key for it.

"What is this?" Ryan asked.

She just shrugged as she rested her hands on the edge of the box. "I don't know. There's no key, or I couldn't find one. I tried to open it with a letter opener, but I couldn't get it to budge."

She could hear Marcus talking and heard the back of the truck open, then the clunk of something that sounded like a ramp being pulled. Ryan rummaged in his pockets, maybe for something to open the box, and finally pulled a key off his keychain. It looked like something for a pair of cuffs.

For a second, as he worked the lock, she wanted him to stop.

"Jenny…" Marcus called out.

She turned and took in the dark man waiting outside, wearing a ballcap and worn jeans. The back of the van was open.

"You want to keep anything here?" he said.

She just took it all in, focusing on the artwork in the corner, which was all wrapped. She knew they were worth something.

Just then, she heard a siren.

"Marcus," the guy called out.

As she followed him outside the storage unit, she took in the scene. Four Atlanta PD cars had pulled up, and cops were stepping out. Marcus was already walking their way, but one of the cops stopped him and held up a paper.

"We have a warrant," one said to her and Ryan. "Please step out of the unit."

Jenny, for the second time in her life, felt a bone-chilling fear at seeing cops. As they stepped into the unit, it hit her that whatever they were looking for could ruin her life or her daughter's.

"What's going on here?" said an approaching detective. Jenny recognized her from the initial investigation—Detective Hargrave, she thought. Her blond hair was cut in a short bob, and she had blue eyes and wore a bulletproof vest over a T-shirt and a holstered gun. She was about the same height as Jenny and was staring right at her.

Meanwhile, Marcus was talking to another cop, and Ryan had walked over to their car. As he closed the door, she wasn't sure what he was doing, but he quickly stepped over beside her and slid his arm around her. She knew the detective didn't miss the motion.

"Since I don't live here anymore, we're cleaning out

the locker," Jenny said. "This is what's left of my husband's things." She wanted to pat herself on the back for sounding so calm even though her heart was hammering. She could feel herself trembling, though, mainly because she still didn't have a clue what was in the boxes. "The question I have, Detective, is why are you here?"

The cops were in the storage unit, and one of them was in the box they had just opened, the one holding dozens of files Wren had kept on the kind of people who had a lot of influence, people who made things happen.

"Detective, over here," one of the cops called out.

Ryan was quiet beside her, just watching the cops in the storage locker.

"Just a minute," was all Hargrave said before heading over.

Jenny was kicking herself for keeping all those papers, files, and God knew what else. It was just one more action that could end up costing her in ways she didn't want to imagine.

Marcus made his way over. "What are they looking at?" he asked her. "What was in that box?"

She shrugged. "Files and stuff Wren had on people, important people… I don't know."

The cops were opening all the boxes, going through one and then another. She couldn't explain what happened next: Hargrave handed one of the files to another cop, who walked out and strode to an unmarked car. Then, as if that was all they needed, all of the cops were leaving.

"Like, what the hell…?" Marcus said under his breath. The glance he exchanged with Ryan conveyed the same confusion she felt. "Detective, can I have a word with you?" he said and started after Hargrave, who was speaking with two of the other cops. She looked over at Jenny.

"I have a bad feeling about this," Jenny said.

"Yeah, well…" was all Ryan replied. The detective started back over to them. Behind her, Marcus was shaking his head.

"We have everything we need," Hargrave said. Then, as if she didn't know what else to say, she asked, "You'll be emptying the rest of the locker?"

"Yes, we will," Ryan said.

Hargrave nodded, and then she and the cops were in their cars, their flashing lights now off as they pulled away.

"What was that about?" Ryan asked.

Marcus appeared frustrated and grim. "All I know is your husband must have had a file on someone pretty important. My guess is that whoever it is has ties to the Atlanta PD, and this is their way of making sure it never sees the light of day."

"So you're saying they weren't looking for something to pin his murder on me or my daughter?" she said. "What about Troy's lawyer?"

Marcus just shook his head and rubbed his hand over the back of his neck. "I've seen a lot of things, but that was one of the strangest. In case they change their minds and decide to come back, let's clean this up. We'll get rid of everything so there's no next time—and if there is something in there, we can make sure it'll never be found."

Chapter 24

"What are you doing inside the house? Everyone's outside," Ryan said, taking in Alison, who was lingering in the living room. They were at his mom's house, and she was in a sundress that stopped just above the knees, soft cotton and sleeveless. He had to remind himself not to tell her how nice she looked. Even though his mom and sisters could, he couldn't, because she was still in that stage of wanting to make his life a living hell if he said anything nice to her.

"Just looking around," she said, touching the figurines on the shelves.

He could hear the laughter from out back, where Owen was barbecuing and Suzanne, Karen, his mom, and Jenny were sitting around the patio table, drinking wine. Marcus was working the night shift, and he couldn't help the ache that filled his gut as he stared at the empty spot on the corner of the sofa where Luke would sit when he was on leave.

Where he was, Ryan didn't know, and he had no idea when he'd be home.

"So you grew up here?" Alison said. "Your mom said you used to get in trouble a lot."

He wasn't sure if he pulled a face as he crossed his arms and stepped into the living room with her, hearing the tick of the old clock on the wall. "My mom shouldn't be sharing all our old horror stories. We were kids, we got in trouble, but we pulled it together," he said. "You went to school today. How was it?"

She just shrugged, and the way she did it seemed so much like her mom. "It's school. It's boring. So, Mom said you're moving in."

There it was. He wondered where her head was on the subject.

"I am. Told you that was the plan. You okay with that?"

"Whatever." She didn't look at him, though he was pretty sure that was code for *That's great.* "You won't hurt my mom, will you?"

He took another step closer to her, then another, seeing the way she stood her ground. "I'm not Wren. I think you know that. I won't hurt you or your mom. Besides, you've seen my family. You think they would let me get away with something like that?"

For the first time, he thought she smiled. She shook her head and rolled her shoulders as if relaxing a bit. "I guess you're right. I like your family."

Had she just complimented him? Kind of, in a way.

"I like my family too, Alison—but in case no one has told you this, they're your family as well."

She nodded and allowed her deep brown eyes to take him in. They turned serious for a second. "You know my dad, I mean, Wren, had things on my mom, on other people…"

He knew she was talking about the files he'd quickly looked through, the ones the cops hadn't taken. The one they had…well, all he knew was that it must've been about someone important. Marcus had said he'd have the rest shredded and burned. The furniture had been donated to Goodwill, and the artwork had been given to the children's hospital. The storage unit was now empty, and there was nothing that could come back on Jenny or Alison.

Then there was the locked box he'd smuggled into the car after the cops arrived. He had opened it up at his house, and he was still sick from the images of shackled naked women he'd found inside. Wren was one sick bastard, and far from the typical asshole.

"I know, but you don't have to worry," he said. "Your uncle Marcus and I took care of everything. You know you can talk to me about anything. Whatever you say to me won't go anywhere. We can talk about Wren, anything you saw that maybe you don't understand…?"

She shrugged, and he could see how uncomfortable she was. "He's dead, but you're not," she said.

The way she looked up to him had him stepping over closer to her, really taking her in. "In case no one told you, Alison, you look really nice."

She rolled her eyes. "Okay, now you're going to ruin it and I'm going to have to change. Mom!" she shouted, then started to walk out of the room, but she stopped just outside the kitchen and looked back to him.

"Hey, I'll take it back if you want me to," he called out. "Seriously, don't be so damn prickly."

She was considering something, and then she glanced over her shoulder to him again, though she didn't turn around, because that would be giving him everything. "In case I didn't say it, I'm glad you're moving in…Dad," she said. Then she left and was out the door in the backyard, and he was stunned.

His pain-in-the-ass teenager had just called him Dad. Things were definitely beginning to look up.

Turn the page for a sneak peek of
THE THIRD CALL the second book in THE O'CONNELLS
Available in print, eBook & audio

The Third Call
THE O'CONNELLS

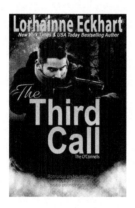

Deputy Marcus O'Connell is blindsided one night after a series of calls comes in from an unknown number, and the caller on the other end is a child. All he knows is she's six years old, her name is Eva, and there's someone in her house who wants to hurt her.

Marcus is the ultimate bad boy turned deputy. He knows everything about how to get away with something, considering he was one of the middle of the six O'Connell siblings. He never had responsibility resting on his shoulders like his brother Owen, and he's never been the center of attention like his little sister, Suzanne. Marcus knows how to find trouble and talk his way out of it.

Now, as the head deputy for the Livingston sheriff's office, he knows everything about everybody, and no one can pull anything over on him. It's why he's such a damn good deputy. But even Marcus dreads what cops know as the third call.

When Marcus takes the call the first time, he thinks it's a prank. The second time, he knows there's a problem. The third time the call comes in and is patched through to him, he knows it's something he can't ignore. The only thing is, the girl is terrified and keeps hanging up, and Marcus knows someone is in the house with her.

Where are her parents, and who is this mysterious girl who needs his help?

The Third Call

CHAPTER 1

Deputy Marcus O'Connell took another swallow of Suzanne's favorite local stout and wondered how his sister could drink the stuff. He'd never taken to heavy dark beer, preferring lighter lagers, and he was drinking it now only because she'd ordered two and slid one over to him just after he got there. Now, she was making her way over to one of the firefighters, Lieutenant Toby Chandler.

"Stop staring at them," said Sheriff Osbert Berry, Bert for short, who was sitting on the same stool at the end of the bar where he always sat, nursing the ale on tap. Marcus hadn't known he was paying attention.

"I'm not staring. I'm observing. There's a difference." He leaned on the bar, having to glance back over his shoulder to Bert, who seemed to have packed on a few more pounds as of late. He already had a hefty frame for a man in his sixties, and it appeared he hadn't shaved in days.

"Bullshit, Marcus," Bert said. "You're staring them down with that look you have that makes everyone nervous. She's flirting, blowing off steam. Let her have some fun, and remember, son, you're talking to the man who wrote the book on staring down numbskulls whose asses you want to kick. I trained you. I know you better than anyone."

For a second, Bert smiled almost fondly over at Suzanne, who he still couldn't believe was making eyes at Toby. Why couldn't she see that his only redeeming quality was the fact that he showed up for work? His sister was one of the best firefighters in Livingston, and if push came to shove, it would be her Marcus wanted saving his ass, not the asshole she was making eyes at.

"I mean, look at him," Marcus said, "the way he looks down at her with that flashy plastic smile he puts on for every girl. Why the hell can't she see the guy's a player, shallow, got nothing going for him? Lost count of the number of times I've told her to look anywhere else. She's been with the department longer, yet he got the promotion to lieutenant last week. Give you three guesses as to why he got it and not her."

He dragged his gaze back down the bar as his sister tossed her hair over her shoulder and shrugged, flirting. He had to look away. The sheriff was softly chuckling under his breath, then polished off the pint in front of him and gestured to Ken, the bartender and owner of the Light-house bar, a silver-haired former golden-gloves fighter and someone else he had to keep an eye on.

"What, you mean just because he's a strapping young white man who has the same last name as the former chief?" Bert said as Ken slid him another pint. He nodded in thanks, then lifted his gaze to Marcus, who was counting the number of pints he'd downed—five or six, he thought. "Take a look in the mirror, son. Some could say the same about you." Bert's blue eyes were bloodshot with the sorrow that seemed to be a part of him now, so many months since he'd put his wife in the ground.

"Seriously, what the hell does that have to do with anything?" Marcus said. "I'm fucking good at what I do, and I didn't step over anyone or have anything handed to me. Doors weren't all that open for me, if you recall."

In fact, he was one of the six O'Connell kids, the brood who had been known as walking trouble—the kind of reputation their mom had warned them would be forever burned in the townsfolk's minds. He had frequently found himself in trouble as a kid, so much so that Bert had taken to picking him up immediately whenever someone did something, just to save time tracking him down. Constantly being one step from juvie had made him pick up on the kinds of things everyone else missed. Whether at accidents or crime scenes, he now had a sixth sense, just knowing who had done what before anyone could even make notes or grab a coffee. Maybe he just knew exactly how someone living a life of crime would think. If he didn't know the who, he just about always knew the why and the how.

The sheriff lifted his hand to stop him. "Just making a point is all, Marcus. You think I don't know all that? Well, what I know doesn't matter. People forget all that when shit hits the fan. We're not all balanced and politically correct and everything—and that kind of thing now matters, as was pointed out to me this morning by the city council." Bert gave him a significant glance.

Marcus gave everything to the old man he'd once looked up to. "What exactly was pointed out and by who?" he said, then looked down at the dark stout. He just couldn't make himself drink it, so he pushed it away. What had his sister been thinking, ordering it for him? Oh, yeah, she'd been distracted over Toby at the other end of the bar. Just then, Toby lifted his chin to Marcus as if they were friends, so he dragged his gaze back over to the sheriff, who leaned on the bar and lifted his pint of ale to take another swallow.

"Oh, you know," Bert said, "the same old crew, the mayor and all his cronies. Apparently, they want to see us more diverse and colorful. We've been told to hire a woman for the open deputy position."

For a second, he wasn't sure he'd heard correctly. "What open deputy position?"

Bert made a face. "The one the city council advised me of. Apparently, the backlog of paperwork and reports, budgets and stuff—ones I supposedly finished, signed, and submitted—showed that for the first time, the sheriff's office is actually in the black when it comes to closing cases. In fact, we're listed among the top fifty offices with the lowest numbers of unsolved crimes, or something along those lines, for whoever comes up with that kind of stuff. Funny thing is, though, I couldn't remember submitting all that paperwork."

Marcus wasn't sure what to say. The sheriff seemed to consider something as he looked around the bar. "Look, Sheriff…" he started before the old man rested his beer on the bar and cut him off.

"I know you've been covering for me," he said. "I know you're the one who's made sure everyone is getting where they need to be, getting the office staffed, giving tickets to keep the revenue coming in, making sure cases are being closed and lines aren't being crossed so this place stays safe. You make sure all the Ts are crossed and no one fucks up anywhere. I knew it was you, always did. In case I haven't said it, thank you. My head hasn't been in it, you know…" He stopped talking, and that sadness returned. So did the knot in Marcus's stomach as he thought of the day the call had come in. Peach Berry had

had a heart attack at the hair salon while getting her roots done. The dye had still been in her hair. His sister had been first on the scene, and he'd been second. He didn't think he'd ever forget the way the old man had cried.

"Stop it," Marcus said. "It's what we do. So we get extra help now? Good. I guess as long as it's someone who can do the job and is qualified…"

Case in point in terms of a lack of qualifications, in his mind, was Toby Chandler at the end of the bar, who was not only flirting openly with his sister but also taking in every hot woman in the room.

His cell phone buzzed, and he pulled it out, seeing the sheriff's office on the screen. "O'Connell," he said. The sheriff was now giving him everything.

"Sorry to bug you, Marcus," said Charlotte Roy, their dispatcher. "I know you're off, but I got a call, a young kid, I think, probably horsing around and stuff. You know how kids get a hold of the phone and play when mom and dad aren't looking. The kid hung up after a few seconds, no number or name. You said to let you know if anything came in."

Charlotte had also been picking up on everything the sheriff had missed. Thirty years old, she was a good woman, a good friend. As a dispatcher, she was the best, but even she would admit that as a wife, she sucked.

"No, that's totally fine, Charlotte," he said. "Anything come up on call display, anything to give you an idea of who the kid is?"

The sheriff had picked up on what he was saying, and he seemed to be fumbling for his wallet, so Marcus quickly gestured to the barman to take his keys.

"Nope, nothing. It's likely one of those burners. The kid was young, only said hi and then hung up. That makes me think it's a kid playing around with the phone, you know?"

As he listened to Charlotte, he took in the back and forth between the bartender and sheriff and knew he was going to have to step in. "Okay, could be right," he said. "Just keep an ear open and call me if anything else comes up. Would be ideal to find out so I can check in and at least give the parents a heads-up that the kid's playing with their phone. You know what? I'll pop back into the station."

He hung up and pocketed his cell phone, then saw his sister making her way back over to him, so he tapped the counter and gestured to the pint of stout she'd ordered for him. "Hey, you can finish that," he said. "I've got to go. You done down there, or you going to continue making a fool of yourself?"

Of course, what did she do but roll her eyes? "Oh, Marcus, seriously, keep your opinions to yourself and your nose out of my business," Suzanne said, settling her own stout on the bar top. Marcus just grunted.

Just then, the sheriff stepped off the stool, and he swayed a bit, keys in hand, while Ken held his palm out, demanding the sheriff turn them over.

"Whoa, there!" Marcus said. "You just give those to me. You're not driving anywhere." He grabbed the keys one handed and tossed them to Ken behind the bar, who stuffed them under the counter. He reached for Bert's arm, taking in the concern on his sister's face.

"You got him?" she said.

In the buzz of the bar, he knew his sister understood everything. Just then, asshole Toby came up and joined her, so Marcus just said, "Yeah, yeah. I got him."

But the sheriff pulled away, staggering to the door. "I can drive myself," he said. "I've been driving myself every-where for longer than you been born…"

Marcus watched a second, listening to the sheriff carry on, then tipped his chin to his sister before following Bert out the door. He grabbed his arm before he could fall over, preparing for the nightly routine: Bert would continue to argue the entire way home, even after he helped him inside the dusty small rancher, put him to bed, and pulled his boots off. He'd be snoring before Marcus left.

Then he'd stop back into the office and check on everything one final time before taking off for the night.

About the Author

"Lorhainne Eckhart is one of my go to authors when I want a guaranteed good book. So many twists and turns, but also so much love and such a strong sense of family."

(Lora W., Reviewer)

New York Times & USA Today bestseller Lorhainne Eckhart writes Raw Relatable Real Romance is best known for her big family romances series, where "Morals and family are running themes. Danger, romance, and a drive to do what is right will see you glued to the page." As one fan calls her, she is the "Queen of the family saga." (aherman) writing "the ups and downs of what goes on within a family but also with some suspense, angst and of course a bit of romance thrown in for good measure." Follow Lorhainne on Bookbub to receive alerts on New Releases and Sales and join her mailing list at LorhainneEckhart.com for her Monday Blog, books news, giveaways and FREE reads. With over 120 books, audiobooks, and multiple series published and available at all retailers now translated into six languages. She is a multiple recipient of the Readers' Favorite Award for Suspense and Romance, and lives in the Pacific Northwest on an island, is the mother of three, her oldest has autism and she is an advocate for never giving up on your dreams.

"Lorhainne Eckhart has this uncanny way of just hitting the spot every time with her books."

(Caroline L., Reviewer)

The O'Connells: *The O'Connells of Livingston, Montana are not your typical family. A riveting collection of stories surrounding the ups and downs of what goes on within a family but also with some suspense, angst and of course a bit of romance thrown in for good measure "I thought I loved the Friessens, but I absolutely adore the O'Connell's. Each and every book has totally different genres of stories but the one thing in common is how she is able to wrap it around the family which is the heart of each story." (C. Logue)*

The Friessens: *An emotional big family romance series, the Friessen family siblings find their relationships tested, lay their hearts on the line, and discover lasting love! "Lorhainne Eckhart is one of my go to authors when I want a guaranteed good book. So many twists and turns, but also so much love and such a strong sense of family." (Lora W., Reviewer)*

The Parker Sisters: *The Parker Sisters are a close-knit family, and like any other family they have their ups and downs. "Eckhart has crafted another intense family drama…The character development is outstanding, and the emotional investment is high…" (Aherman, Reviewer)*

The McCabe Brothers: *Join the five McCabe siblings on their journeys to the dark and dangerous side of love! An intense, exhilarating collection of romantic thrillers you won't want to miss. — "Eckhart has a new series that is definitely worth the read. The queen of the family saga started this series with a spin-off of her wildly successful Friessen series." From a Readers' Favorite award—winning author and "queen of the family saga" (Aherman)*

Lorhainne loves to hear from her readers! You can connect with me at:
www.LorhainneEckhart.com
lorhainneeckhart.le@gmail.com

Also by Lorhainne Eckhart

The Outsider Series
The Forgotten Child (Brad and Emily)
A Baby and a Wedding *(An Outsider Series Short)*
Fallen Hero (Andy, Jed, and Diana)
The Search *(An Outsider Series Short)*
The Awakening (Andy and Laura)
Secrets (Jed and Diana)
Runaway (Andy and Laura)
Overdue *(An Outsider Series Short)*
The Unexpected Storm (Neil and Candy)
The Wedding (Neil and Candy)

The Friessens: A New Beginning
The Deadline (Andy and Laura)
The Price to Love (Neil and Candy)
A Different Kind of Love (Brad and Emily)
A Vow of Love, A Friessen Family Christmas

The Friessens
The Reunion
The Bloodline (Andy & Laura)
The Promise (Diana & Jed)
The Business Plan (Neil & Candy)
The Decision (Brad & Emily)
First Love (Katy)
Family First
Leave the Light On
In the Moment

In the Family
In the Silence
In the Charm
Unexpected Consequences
It Was Always You
The First Time I Saw You
Welcome to My Arms
Welcome to Boston
I'll Always Love You
Ground Rules
A Reason to Breathe
You Are My Everything
Anything For You
The Homecoming
Stay Away From My Daughter
The Bad Boy
A Place of Our Own
The Visitor
All About Devon
Long Past Dawn
How to Heal a Heart
Keep Me in Your Heart

The O'Connells

The Neighbor
The Third Call
The Secret Husband
The Quiet Day
The Commitment
The Missing Father
The Hometown Hero
Justice
The Family Secret

The Fallen O'Connell
The Return of the O'Connells
And The She Was Gone
The Stalker
The O'Connell Family Christmas
The Girl Next Door

The McCabe Brothers
Don't Stop Me (Vic)
Don't Catch Me (Chase)
Don't Run From Me (Aaron)
Don't Hide From Me (Luc)
Don't Leave Me (Claudia)
Out of Time

A Billy Jo McCabe Mystery
Nothing As it Seems
Hiding in Plain Sight
The Cold Case
The Trap
Above the Law

The Wilde Brothers
The One (Joe and Margaret)
The Honeymoon, A Wilde Brothers Short
Friendly Fire (Logan and Julia)
Not Quite Married, A Wilde Brothers Short
A Matter of Trust (Ben and Carrie)
The Reckoning, A Wilde Brothers Christmas
Traded (Jake)
Unforgiven (Samuel)
The Holiday Bride

Married in Montana
His Promise
Love's Promise
A Promise of Forever

The Parker Sisters
Thrill of the Chase
The Dating Game
Play Hard to Get
What We Can't Have
Go Your Own Way
A June Wedding

Kate & Walker
One Night
Edge of Night
Last Night

Walk the Right Road Series
The Choice
Lost and Found
Merkaba
Bounty
Blown Away: The Final Chapter

The Saved Series
Saved
Vanished
Captured

Single Titles
He Came Back
Loving Christine

For my German Readers
Die Außenseiter-Reihe
Der Vergessene Junge
Der Gefallene Held

For my French Readers
L'ENFANT OUBLIÉ

Printed in Great Britain
by Amazon